Here'
th

MW01519401

"Elizabeth Ashby and Gin Jones piece together the perfect holiday who-dunnit. I suggest you pick this one up and treat yourself to a merry murder this Christmas. Top Pick!"
~ *Night Owl Reviews*

"High-octane entertainment and doesn't dip into a lull for even a sec! 5 stars!"
~ *Long Island Book Review*

"I am a frequent visitor to Danger Cove, and eager to stay for a long time. The mystery is very clever... put your inner Sherlock into high gear! Mixing it with some personal peril leads readers to a great conclusion...Loved it!"
~ *Kings River Life Magazine*

"The Danger Cove series continues to entertain as it showcases the talent of the GHP writers. This book is a keeper...I highly recommend this book!"
~ *Authors on the Air*

DANGER COVE BOOKS

Secret of the Painted Lady
Murder & Mai Tais
Death by Scones
Patchwork of Death
Deadly Dye & a Soy Chai
Killer Clue at the Ocean View
A Christmas Quilt to Die For
"A Killing in the Market"
(short story in the Killer Beach Reads collection)
Killer Colada
Passion, Poison, & Puppy Dogs
A Novel Death
Clues in Calico
Sinister Snickerdoodles
Heroes & Hurricanes
A Death in the Flower Garden
Divas, Diamonds & Death
A Slaying in the Orchard
A Secret in the Pumpkin Patch
Deadly Dirty Martinis
A Poison Manicure & Peach Liqueur
"Not-So-Bright Hopes"
(short story in the Pushing Up Daisies collection)
Tequila Trouble
Deadly Thanksgiving Sampler
Killer Eyeshadow & a Cold Espresso
Two Sleuths Are Better Than One
Dark Rum Revenge
Cozy Room With a Killer View

A CHRISTMAS QUILT TO DIE FOR

a Danger Cove mystery

Gin Jones &
Elizabeth Ashby

This book is dedicated to Kathi, who kept insisting that Keely's story needed to be told.

CHAPTER ONE

———

The Christmas season always brought out the perfectionist in me.

In the past, my need to make everything perfect had made me an effective and highly sought-after trial attorney. Even after my forced retirement, it came in useful in my detail-oriented work as a quilt appraiser. But it had its down side too, contributing to my syncope, a medical condition that caused me to pass out in stressful situations.

With practice, I'd learned to not sweat the little things, but there were times when my old habits threatened to get the better of me. Like today. I was on my way to the Danger Cove Historical Museum, where I would be part of an ornament-making workshop. It was the kickoff for the entire holiday season at the museum, and today's success—I refused to consider any other possibility—would set the tone for the rest of the month. The museum was the biggest client for my fledgling appraisal business, and its director was a friend, so I had both professional and personal reasons for wanting today's event to go well.

The weather was cooperating, at least. The sky was clear and bright. The storefronts were decorated with a variety of winter holiday displays, and the sidewalks were filled with happy tourists searching the trendy little downtown shop windows for just the right gifts or getting themselves a treat at The Clip and Sip, where the beauty salon's clientele got a free drink with each service. Even the Main Street trolley was festive, sporting a wreath at each end of the car and tiny red-and-white LED lights outlining the windows.

I contributed in a small way to the holiday decor, with my dark-green jeans, lightweight green tweed sweater, and a red ribbon that tied back my shoulder-length hair. Over my shoulder, I carried a quilted messenger bag filled to overflowing. I'd packed, unpacked, and repacked it at least a dozen times last night to make sure I didn't forget any of my paperwork or reference books. The new owner of the local bookstore had even managed to get me a pristine copy of Marsha McCloskey's *Christmas Quilts*, which had pictures of a wide variety of holiday quilts to help with identifying designs. I checked once again, confirming that it was in my bag. It would have been a shame to forget it after all of Meri Sinclair's effort to get it for me in time for today's event.

I was determined that there wouldn't be any hitches today, no matter how minor. I used to be good in a crisis, but my career as a civil trial lawyer had apparently used up all of my allotted ability to withstand stress by the time I reached the age of thirty-six. That was two years ago, when I'd been diagnosed with syncope and quit my job to seek a quieter life as Keely Fairchild, quilt appraiser.

At least, that had been the plan. I'd almost been killed shortly after moving to Danger Cove, while looking into the murder of a shady quilt dealer. Everyone had been so kind and supportive afterward that I'd never given a single serious thought to leaving Danger Cove. The last three months had been every bit as peaceful and relaxing as I'd hoped for, and my new business was growing steadily.

At the museum's entrance, I glanced up at the sign high on the brick facade. Yesterday, while everyone else in town had been indulging in Black Friday shopping, the museum's director, Gil Torres, had joined a coalition of Main Street merchants who thought *Danger* Cove was a little off-putting for the holiday tourists, and she had overseen the installation of a temporary sign that read *Christmas Cove Historical Museum*. It looked as official as the real sign, which wasn't surprising. Gil was as much of a perfectionist as I was, and the museum was her entire life, much like my legal practice had once been mine.

Upstairs in the museum's boardroom, which was sometimes used for community events, another transformation had taken place. The only permanent furniture in the high-ceilinged, warehouse-like space—a huge conference table that seated eighteen people—had been shoved against the wall across from the entrance, beneath the large windows overlooking Main Street, and the chairs had been lined up along the opposite wall. The rest of the 30-foot by 50-foot room had then been filled with what amounted to an assembly line for making quilted ornaments. Closest to the heavy, oversized double doors was a ten-foot-long banquet table topped with cutting mats, acrylic rulers, rotary cutters, and sunshine-yellow-handled scissors. Beyond the table was a white board and then a square table in the corner. In the middle of the room, four more banquet tables held three sewing machines each, with yellow-handled scissors placed to the right of each machine. Ironing boards were scattered throughout the room. Volunteers—mostly women, but I counted two men and one Labradoodle wearing a service vest—scurried around, unpacking boxes of red-and-green fabric and notions and distributing them to the appropriate tables. Danger Cove's most famous resident, mystery author Elizabeth Ashby, wandered around the room. She carried a notebook with a seasonally appropriate red-and-green plaid cover and stopped occasionally to jot down her observations of the event. That should have been the job of the local arts reporter, Matt Viera, but he'd been missing in action for a while.

No one paid me any attention, and I didn't know where I was supposed to set up my appraisal station. I'm tall, but the museum's director is a good three inches beyond my five foot nine inches, so even in the bustling activity, it was easy to spot Gil Torres. She was near the conference table under the windows, talking to a woman I didn't recognize.

The stranger appeared to be around sixty, with platinum blonde hair and wearing a Santa hat and a red-and-white pinafore-style apron. From time to time, Gil couldn't resist singing along with the James Taylor holiday CD playing in the background. She took the Natalie Cole part, lamenting how cold it was outside, even though the coast was actually experiencing typical mild Pacific Northwest weather for late November, which definitely didn't present any risk of hypothermia or frostbite.

In keeping with the holiday season, Gil wore a forest-green blouse with a hand-knit burgundy shawlette that was perfect with her dark skin. Even from a distance, I could tell that she was bubbling over with enthusiasm for being inside the bright, warm museum with about twenty of her very best friends and with the anticipation of another ten or twenty such close friends stopping by before the end of the day.

This was Gil's first Christmas as the director of the museum, and she was going all out. She'd recently acquired an anonymous major donor for the museum, so she had some cash to establish a few new and ambitious holiday traditions. One of them was the acquisition of a massive evergreen to be installed in the lobby and covered with dozens of little wooden lighthouses painted red and white like the one overlooking Danger Cove, and an equal number of miniature red-and-white quilts, each just three or four inches square, that were being made today.

All we needed now was enough volunteers to make the ornaments. That was why I was here, offering an informal appraisal of a holiday quilt in return for a nominal donation to the museum, which would be waived for anyone who made an ornament. Fortunately, the success of the event wasn't entirely on my shoulders. Gil had also hired a nationally recognized quilting teacher for the day to motivate both quilting novices and the more experienced members of the Danger Cove Quilt Guild to come and make ornaments.

The Santa-hatted woman said something to Gil and then dashed across the room and past me, out the double doors I had just come through.

Gil approached me at a more normal pace, singing along with the sound system. She gave me a quick hug, and when the music ended, said, "You can use the board secretary's desk in the back corner to do appraisals. It's been cleared off, and you'll be out of the way there, so you won't be distracted by all the activity of the quilters."

I looked at the spot where she was pointing. The top of the heavy wood desk was cleared of everything except for a swing-arm lamp that lit the otherwise gloomy corner, too far away from the windows to take advantage of the bright sunshine.

Beside the desk was an easel with a sign proclaiming that one Keely Fairchild, certified quilt appraiser, would be there from 10 a.m. to noon today. I wasn't scheduled to start for another fifteen minutes—showing up early for appointments was another leftover habit from my days of practicing law—but there was already a line of five people seated in the chairs near the back table, with red-and-green quilts on their laps.

"Do I need to remind people that only holiday quilts are eligible for appraisal today? Or make sure they've paid by making an ornament or donating to the museum?"

"Oh, no," Gil said. "It's all taken care of. One of the women from the quilt guild is in charge of that. She'll give everyone who qualifies for an appraisal a ticket to give to you as proof of eligibility."

"You did warn them that I'm just giving a superficial overview, right?"

"Of course," Gil said. "If you think the quilt is valuable enough to need insurance, you can always encourage them to hire you to do a full appraisal later. I'm just hoping we can find some more works eligible for the museum's registry of locally made quilts. Do you have the documentation sheets for that?"

"I do." I patted my bulging messenger bag. Another person joined the line waiting for me. "I'd better get to work, or I won't be able to do even a cursory examination of all the quilts before the end of my session."

"I hope you'll stay for a while afterwards and make some ornaments with us."

"Oh, no," I said. "Dee has been trying to get me to learn to quilt, but I know my limits. No way I'm ever getting behind the controls of a sewing machine. I haven't trusted anything with sharp edges and fast-moving parts since my first year of law school. Reading the product liability cases in a torts class textbook completely changes how you look at household appliances. Ignorance truly is bliss when it comes to knowing about all the accidents that can happen with seemingly harmless products like toasters, vacuum cleaners, and sewing machines."

"I think I'll stay ignorant then." Gil hummed along with the next song playing in the background. "Just let me know if you need anything else for your appraisals."

The Santa-hatted woman who'd dashed out of the room returned and gathered most of the volunteers, including Gil, together near the white board at the front of the room. Only two women stayed where they were in the back of the room. One was the frail, eighty-three-year-old president of the Danger Cove Quilt Guild, Dee Madison, who was seated at a sewing machine in the last row of tables. The other was Dee's decade-younger and much sturdier friend, Emma Quinn, hovering at Dee's shoulder to do her bidding.

I couldn't put names to any of the volunteers at the white board, although I'd probably met most of them in passing at the local quilt show this past summer. Not the male quilter with the service dog though. I'd have remembered them, since both men and dogs were underrepresented in the quilting world.

The Santa-hatted woman had to be the quilting instructor, Meg McLaughlin. It looked like she was making sure everyone understood the plan for the day. The white board had little drawings of the miniature quilt blocks they'd be making today, along with the dimensions for cutting the pieces for each block. I knew a great deal more about the value of finished quilts than about how they were made, and, in other circumstances, I'd have been interested in hearing what Meg had to say. But even as I considered listening in for a couple of minutes, another person with a quilt to be appraised joined the line waiting for me.

I hurried over to unload the reference books and the paperwork from my quilted messenger bag. As I set up, the group at the white board dispersed, and one of the only other people I knew by name, Stefan Anderson, scurried over to claim the ironing board closest to me. He was a slight man in his early thirties, wearing Benjamin Franklin-style glasses. His bow tie was a festive red-and-green plaid, and for once the overlong sleeves of his pale, buttoned-down shirt had been folded up to his elbows instead of being allowed to slide past his wrists to cover his knuckles. Some things never changed though, and the hems of his khaki pants dragged on the wood floor.

Stefan must have closed his folk-art gallery for the morning. That wasn't as much of a sacrifice as it might seem, since he did most of his business in the summer, and his major deals, the ones that netted most of his profit, were by appointment only. As far as I knew, Stefan wasn't a quilter, but he was always welcome at the museum, both for his successful brokering of some recent additions to the museum's quilt collection and for his extensive knowledge of the museum's collection of folk art. He sometimes led tours at the museum and enjoyed sharing his extensive knowledge in excruciating detail with anyone who didn't run away from him.

I didn't recognize the stocky, black-haired woman at his side, who appeared to be lecturing Stefan, forcing him to do the listening for a change. Her smooth round face made it difficult to pinpoint her age, but if I had to guess, I'd have said she was at least five years older than Stefan, maybe more. She wore jeans and a red turtleneck covered with a handmade green smock decorated with what Dee and Emma would have called "cheater cloth." The fabric was printed with scaled reproductions of miniature quilts, which could then be cut apart and appliquéd like the woman in the smock had done, or simply layered and finished to make a quilt without having to actually piece together all the little bits of fabric.

Just as I was about to call over the first person for her appraisal, a tall, willowy blonde in her early twenties, and wearing a pink twinset and heathery purple jeans, came trotting over from the white board. "I'm Trudy Kline," she said. "Emma sent me over to help you."

I handed her the appraisal forms and pencils so she could distribute them to the women seated in the line of chairs along the wall. While they waited, they could fill out the top portion of the forms with their names and addresses and any other background information they had about their quilts.

I called the first client over to the desk and soon lost myself in the work. The first quilt was a faded green-and-white version of a traditional appliqué design known as Oak Leaf. It wasn't terribly old, maybe fifty years, but the workmanship was excellent, as close to perfection as any human being could get, so I quickly checked the box to suggest that the owner get a full appraisal and insurance. The quilt's owner left with one of my business cards, promising to call for an appointment.

Over the next hour, Trudy kept the line supplied with forms and pencils, while a wide variety of holiday quilts passed through my cotton-gloved hands. They ranged from contemporary quilts using fabrics printed with obvious holiday motifs, to vintage quilts that, like the first Oak Leaf, were red and green but didn't otherwise have any holiday references in either the fabrics or the patterns. There were simple nine-patches, more complicated star designs, and even a vintage Sunbonnet Sue variation in which Santa and his elves all wore sunbonnets.

It had been easy enough to identify the various quilt patterns this morning, but there were other challenges with a holiday quilt, especially the ones that weren't brand new. They were likely to have become something more than an object and instead were a symbol of family memories, including lost loved ones who could no longer join in holiday festivities. Oftentimes these sentimental quilts were unremarkable from any objective viewpoint, so while it was simple enough to come up with a dollar amount, it was far more difficult to explain to the owner why the number was so low. Anything less than an astronomical price tag was often considered a slur against the memories that the quilt represented.

I hadn't encountered that type of reaction so far this morning, but it was probably just a matter of time before the pleasant perfection of the morning turned a little rocky. I just hoped that when the inevitable emotional scene arose, I'd be able to handle it without passing out. The local ambulances might be red and white, but they definitely lacked the Christmas spirit.

* * *

As my latest client prepared to leave, I looked up to see who was next in line. It was a man in his early twenties, dressed in a light T-shirt, cargo shorts, and sandals.

Trudy glanced at him, her eyes narrowing in obvious recognition. She froze for a moment before blocking him from approaching the desk, keeping her back to him. "Emma said you need to take a break now."

I'd been too wrapped up in the appraisals to notice until then that my stomach was growling. Ever since I'd been diagnosed with syncope, I'd tried to pay better attention to my body's various warning signs. The general medical consensus was that stress was the major culprit in the condition, but no one knew the exact cause. To be on the safe side, I'd been warned not to risk dehydration or hunger, either of which might trigger a stress response and then the loss of consciousness.

I could definitely use a break, but I could also feel trouble brewing, and I was the most likely candidate to diffuse it. Behind Trudy and the appraisal client, the male quilter I hadn't been introduced to yet was closing in on our corner of the room. He was an inch or two over six feet tall, solidly built, with faded brown hair and a neatly trimmed beard that was equal parts gray and brown. Tiny snippets of red-and-green threads clung to his denim work shirt and jeans, giving them a festive appearance at odds with his facial expression, which promised the complete opposite of goodwill toward men. Close behind him was the rust-colored Labradoodle, wearing a blue vest that identified it as a Diabetes Alert Dog. He had a matching blue collar, and hanging from it was a stuffed blue nylon tube the size of a chew toy.

The newcomer walked up to the young man behind Trudy, invading his space and glaring down at him. "What are *you* doing here?"

"It's a free country," the younger man said sulkily and then sniffled. "You've got no authority here. No authority anywhere anymore. So butt out, or I'll call the cops on you. That'd be pretty funny, actually. Don't you think?"

"Not really." The older man pulled back a few inches, just to the very edge of an appropriate conversational distance. "I'll be watching you. Don't touch anything that doesn't belong to you. I've still got friends on the force."

"Whatever." The young man peered at me over Trudy's shoulder.

The older man retreated a few feet to lean against the end of the nearest sewing table, where Dee and Emma were seated. He made an *I'm watching you* gesture at the younger man, adjusted the water bottle clipped to his belt, and settled in for what he obviously considered to be a one-man stakeout.

CHAPTER TWO

———

"Maybe I'd better do this one last appraisal before I take a break," I told Trudy.

"But Emma said you had to do it now." Trudy shook her wrist nervously, setting a charm bracelet to rattling. "She's going to yell at me if you don't."

"I'll take care of Emma when I'm done here." I knew Emma Quinn, and she didn't yell at anyone. That was part of her magic. She could organize and supervise every detail of a quilt show, even after being falsely accused of murder, without ever losing her calm demeanor. If I could ever figure out how she maintained her even temperament, I might be able to return to my law practice. "For now, why don't you go take a long bathroom break? By the time you return, I'll be done with this appraisal and ready to take my own break."

Trudy gave me a grateful look then turned toward the exit, coming face to face with the young man waiting for his appraisal. Apparently she hadn't realized how close she was to him, because she started and sidled a few feet away before telling him he could go on over to my table. Then she announced to the remaining half-dozen people in line that I'd be taking a five-minute break as soon as I finished this appraisal, so everyone should go over to get some refreshments at the conference table.

The young man remained standing while he handed me the form he'd completed. He was excruciatingly thin, which made his lightweight summer clothing even more inappropriate. The weather might be mild for the time of year, but it was still the end of November, not August, and he didn't have even the slightest layer of fat that might have made him less susceptible to a chill. I knew people didn't catch a cold simply from being chilled, but I'd heard him sniffling for the last fifteen minutes, and I couldn't help thinking he'd never get better if he continued to dress so inappropriately for the weather.

I glanced at the completed form he'd handed me. "Is this right? The quilt belongs to Georgia Miller? Or did you mean that it was made by someone with that name?"

"No, it belongs to her." His speech was rapid and clipped even though his eyes drooped with fatigue. "My grandmother. I'm Alan Miller. She doesn't get out much these days."

He dropped into the seat across from me, bouncing his knee up and down restlessly. I was no expert, but between the sniffling, the lack of other signs of a respiratory infection, and the restlessness, I had to wonder if he was under the influence of something other than the common cold. The sooner he was done here, the better.

"You left most of the form blank," I said. "It helps to know a bit about the quilt's history. Did your grandmother tell you anything about who made it or when?"

"She doesn't really talk about it, and I didn't have time to ask before I left this morning," he said between sniffles. "I just know she really likes it. I thought she might want to know what it was worth. All official and everything. It's my Christmas gift to her."

It was a heartwarming story, but not the first one I'd heard today. Besides, I couldn't help wondering how much of it was true. All of my training, as both a lawyer and an appraiser, made me a bit of a skeptic when it came to unproven claims. There was at least one other obvious explanation for his ignorance about the quilt: that he'd stolen it, perhaps to sell to feed a drug habit, and he wanted to know how much it was worth before he put it on the black market.

There was always a risk, especially when doing low-cost appraisals, that I was inadvertently abetting a crime. In that sense, being an appraiser came with some of the same stress I'd had as a lawyer. Before taking on a personal injury case, I'd always had to consider whether the client was lying about how he'd been injured or how badly he was hurt in order to defraud an insurance company or government program. At least with quilts, the risk was relatively small compared to the harm caused by a false personal injury claim.

I might be able to tell more during the process of appraising the quilt. I spread it out on the desk so I could see the whole thing. Regardless of who owned it, the quilt was a masterpiece. It was about six feet square, made up of only five large blocks on point, surrounded by a row of triangles that formed a sawtooth border. The blocks were a traditional design known as the Tree of Life, in which rows of dark and light triangles made up the leaves and branches of the tree.

During my training, I'd seen several Tree of Life quilts, but none quite like this one. For obvious reasons, the design was often made out of green prints on a white background, so it was no surprise that this quilt was predominantly green and white. What set it apart though was the random placement of occasional red triangles, like little ornaments, in the trees.

If I needed any additional confirmation that the quilt had been intended for use during the holiday season, I found it in the holly wreaths hand-quilted into the large, white triangles set between the pieced blocks and the outer border. One of the wreaths had a date, 1968, quilted into it, along with what I thought were the initials SM. Quilted letters were often difficult to decipher, but I was absolutely sure the first one wasn't a *G*. Alan's grandmother might be the current owner of the quilt, but she wasn't its maker.

Frequently, a masterpiece-quality quilt, especially one with a holiday theme, was saved for special occasions and used gently, but this one had been used hard. There were stains and broken seams, and some of the greens had faded.

"Well?" Alan said. "What's it worth?"

"This isn't an easy quilt to appraise," I said honestly. "There are a number of pluses and minuses here. The craftsmanship in getting all these triangle points to be so sharp, and in the hand quilting, is extraordinary, which is a plus. Holiday quilts tend to be sought after, so that's a plus too."

He sniffled. "What's the bad news?"

"The design isn't rare, and the quilt is less than a hundred years old. Both of those factors reduce the price a collector might pay. The biggest problem is that the quilt has considerable wear and tear. Just like with other collectibles, items that are new in the box, or otherwise in pristine condition, tend to be more valuable than the ones that have obviously been used."

"My grandmother says quilts get better with use."

"That's true in personal and emotional terms," I said. "Not so much in financial terms. Of course, your grandmother isn't likely to sell something she's so attached to, so what really matters is the enjoyment she gets from it."

"Maybe this wasn't such a good idea." Alan pulled the quilt toward him, preparing to leave.

"Bringing the quilt here was definitely a good idea." I pointed at the quilted initials. "If you can find out who those initials belong to, the quilt might qualify for a program to recognize the quilts made by residents of Danger Cove. All you need to do is fill out the registry form, and your grandmother's quilt will be part of history with its information and a picture maintained here at the museum forever."

"Yeah?" He stopped trying to roll the quilt into a ball. "Do I have to pay anything extra for the honor? I spent all my spare cash to get here, and jobs are scarce these days."

"No, it's free. All we need is for you to find out the rest of the information for the documentation form. We'd also need your contact information since you're the one who brought it in, so we can arrange for it to be professionally photographed."

I was expecting him to come up with another excuse, but he shrugged and said, "Cool. Do I get something to show my grandmother that she's in the registry? She'd like that a lot. Better than the appraisal, even."

I relaxed, and my smile was genuine. I was convinced, at least by a preponderance of the evidence if not all the way beyond a reasonable doubt, that Alan really was just a thoughtful grandson trying to do something nice for his grandmother. Okay, so maybe he also had a drug problem, but at least I probably wasn't contributing to the theft of a quilt.

* * *

After I helped Alan fold up his grandmother's quilt and gave him the envelope with the appraisal, he tried to call a friend to pick him up, but most of the museum was a phone service dead zone. I suggested he'd have better luck out in the parking lot, and if he wanted to leave the quilt with me while he ran outside, I'd keep it safe for him.

Alan left, and I looked for Trudy, but she'd taken full advantage of her bathroom break and hadn't returned yet, so I couldn't ask her to watch over his quilt for me. I stayed at the appraisal desk, sorting the forms I'd collected so far. Several were for the registry of locally made quilts, and I needed to hand them off to the museum's director. I surveyed the room, but Gil must have left, perhaps to deal with something in the exhibit halls, which were open today until 8:00 p.m. Saturdays were a relatively busy day for the museum, after all, even apart from the special events like today's in the boardroom.

Alan returned a few minutes later to reclaim his grandmother's quilt and thank me again.

"Did you reach your friend?" I asked.

He nodded. "He's busy and can't leave for about half an hour, but waiting is better than walking home." He glanced at the older man who'd confronted him earlier and was glowering at him now. "Don't worry. I'll wait outside. I know when I'm not wanted."

Alan wouldn't literally freeze to death out there, but he wouldn't be comfortable in his light clothes. Still, it was probably best if he didn't linger here in the boardroom. When Alan had left to make his call, the older man in the denim shirt had claimed a sewing machine near the front of the room, but now he was turned around, making good on his promise to keep an eye on Alan. "Do you want a box to put the quilt in to make it easier to carry? I'm sure the quilt guild can spare one for you."

"Probably a good idea, huh?" he said. "So it doesn't lose any more value from wear and tear."

I was running out of time to get a snack before I needed to return to do the last few appraisals, so I couldn't help him with the box. I knew who could though. I pointed him in the direction of Emma Quinn, who was still hovering beside her friend Dee at the table closest to me. "Emma can help you. Just tell her I sent you, and she'll take care of it."

Alan headed over to talk to Emma, the quilt tucked under one arm and the appraisal paperwork safely secured inside a buttoned pocket of his cargo shorts. He passed Stefan, who was being dragged over to my corner of the room by the stocky, black-haired woman who'd been lecturing him earlier. Stefan stopped halfway to my table and turned to watch Alan until the woman at Stefan's side snapped something in a tone too low for me to hear.

"Sorry," Stefan said to the woman, and they continued over to my desk. "Was that Alan Miller with a raggedy Tree of Life quilt?"

I nodded. "He was getting it appraised for his grandmother. Do you know him?"

"A little," Stefan said. "Mostly just by reputation. His family has lived here forever, and they have a long history of underachievement. Judging by the way he's dressed today, I'm guessing he's living down to the family reputation. Too bad, really. I thought he was going to be the one to break the family curse. Got a scholarship to the University of Washington, Tacoma, did well there, and then I don't know what happened, but it doesn't look like he's made anything of himself."

The woman at Stefan's side finally spoke, in a fierce whisper addressed to Stefan. "Introduce us."

"Oh, sorry," he said. "Keely Fairchild, this is my girlfriend, Sunny Kunik."

I hesitated. Everyone I'd ever discussed it with believed that Stefan's girlfriend was largely a figment of his imagination. We knew she was a real person—Dee and Emma had told me about her plans to open a quilt shop here in Danger Cove—but it seemed unlikely that Stefan actually had a relationship with her. No one could be as perfect as he'd described her, and if he'd spent more than ten minutes with her, he'd know she was as human as the rest of us.

But here she was, standing next to Stefan and acting very much like a girlfriend. Sunny was about the same height as Stefan, who was shorter than the average man, but she was stockier than his slight build. Her expression was more cloudy than her name would suggest, and her round face, coupled with her last name, suggested she had Inuit blood. Her black hair was long and thick, pulled back in a complicated braid that fell down to her waist. One ear had a whole row of piercings, each hole featuring a different sewing notion: scissors, thread, and even a tiny rotary cutter.

"I'm so glad to meet you finally," I said, finally recovering from my surprise. "I've heard so much about you."

"Likewise," Sunny said, and I had to wonder if the woman had similarly doubted Stefan's stories about me, since they had to have sounded far-fetched, given my recent experience with a homicide investigation.

"I need to go back to my shop for a few minutes," Sunny continued, "but I wanted to make sure to meet you first, in case you have to leave before I get back. Maybe you could come over for dinner with Stefan and me sometime?"

"I'd like that. Just let me know when. Stefan's got my contact information."

"Gotta run," Sunny said. "We're out of batting, and I've got some scraps at the shop that would be perfect for a little project like these ornaments. I should have thought to bring them this morning, but this way I can check on my staff while I'm there."

"Stefan told me you were looking for the right location for your quilt shop," I said. "I didn't realize it was open yet."

"Since the beginning of November. There wasn't any suitable space available here on Main Street, so I settled for a spot near the pier, in the old cannery. The local quilters know where it is, and it's not hard for the tourists to find, even if it's not quite as visible as it would be here in the center of town." Sunny gave Stefan a quick kiss on the check. "I've really got to go. Nice meeting you, Keely."

Sunny took off at top walking speed, almost colliding with Alan at the exit. He hugged his boxed-up quilt to his chest, took a step back, and made an exaggerated half bow to encourage Sunny to precede him through the doorway. He said something, and Sunny responded, but they were too far away for me to hear the exchange. Something about Alan's behavior had upset her though, judging from the stiff way she brushed past him.

Alan followed her, and a moment later, the *Cove Chronicles'* arts reporter, Matt Viera, came in through the double doors and paused to take in the crowd. He was a little taller than the statuesque Gil, but not as massive as the denim-shirted quilter who'd confronted Alan Miller earlier. Matt wore his usual style of cargo pants that had more than the standard number of pockets. I knew from past experience that he could indeed manage to find a use for each and every one of those pockets. His sport shirt was an ochre that clashed with every conceivable shade of human skin and probably every inhuman skin too. Only Matt could wear it without looking deathly ill.

Elizabeth Ashby stopped him to chat for a moment. She headed out, and Matt remained in the doorway, apparently searching the room for something. A moment later, before he'd found whatever he was looking for, the quilt teacher approached the doorway. Matt said something to her, and for a moment I thought she was going to ignore him. She gave the exit a brief but longing look before smiling and letting Matt escort her over to the refreshment table. It seemed that no woman could ever resist his charm. I'd even been susceptible before I'd learned that he couldn't be trusted to follow through on his promises.

I forced my attention back to Stefan. "Sunny seems very...efficient."

"She is." Stefan was still staring dreamily in the direction where Sunny had last been visible. "I don't deserve her, but if she has any flaw at all, it's that she doesn't realize how hopeless I am."

I'd heard him rhapsodize about Sunny before, much like he did when talking about folk art. If he got started talking about her, he'd never stop, and I needed to get something to eat before I passed out. To distract him, I said, "Have you seen Gil? I need to give her some quilt-registry forms."

"I think she had some stuff to do in her office. I was going to spend this morning at my gallery catching up on paperwork myself, but Sunny thought I should be here with her. It's her first community event since opening the quilt shop, so she was a little nervous. She shouldn't have been. Everyone loves her. She donated a lot of the tools for today's use, you know." Stefan pointed at the cutting tables. "The mats and rulers and rotary cutters are all on loan from the shop. The scissors too. They're sort of her trademark. She had them made specially with the sunny-yellow handles."

"Donating all those supplies was very kind of her."

"Smart too. She's getting some good publicity for the shop, narrowly directed to her target audience of quilters, and it doesn't really cost her anything except a few replacement blades for the cutters." Stefan glanced at the ironing board where he'd been stationed earlier. "I'd better get back to work. The blocks are piling up."

I went with him, since it was on the way to the refreshment table. I didn't have time for any real sustenance, but I needed something to get me through the last twenty minutes of appraisal work before my part in today's event was done.

As we reached the ironing board, the quilt teacher in the Santa hat beckoned for a woman, who was apparently her assistant for the day, to come over to take her place with Matt. As the teacher headed for the exit at top speed, she muttered, "'Scuse me. 'Scuse me. 'Scuse me. Stupid overactive bladder. 'Scuse me. 'Scuse me. 'Scuse me."

"Meg's been running to the ladies' room every two minutes," Stefan said. "Don't they have treatments for that?"

I had known Stefan long enough to know that he wasn't being as judgmental as it sounded. He was honestly perplexed whenever people failed to take whatever steps he thought would help them live up to their full potential. He worked very hard at being the best folk art dealer in the county, possibly the entire state, and he expected everyone else to know what their goals were and then to go after them with all their energy and passion. It was why he tended to bristle around his childhood friend, Matt Viera, accusing Matt of frittering away all of his considerable talents. Matt had once been a highly sought-after fashion model and had quit at the peak of his popularity to become an underpaid and underappreciated arts reporter.

As if Stefan could read my mind, he said, "Have you talked to Matt today? He was supposed to be here early to do a story on the event. We were hoping he'd mention Sunny and the Sunny Patches Quilt Shop."

"I didn't even know he was going to be here." I hadn't talked to Matt Viera since the opening luncheon for the Danger Cove Quilt Show in August, when I'd given the keynote speech, and he'd been in the audience. Before that, we'd worked together to find a killer, so he'd been at my home—an abandoned bank branch that had been converted into a residence and home office—and had been fascinated by the idea of the bank vault that I'd kept during the renovation. I'd promised to give him a tour, and he'd said he'd call. Over the course of the next three months of silence though, I'd come to accept that his flirting during the investigation had just been part of his job as a reporter, nothing personal. Once he'd had his scoop for the *Cove Chronicles*, he'd completely lost interest in the bank vault and me. It had hurt, but it wasn't like he'd ended a real relationship. We'd barely gotten to know each other, after all, even if it had felt like more than a brief acquaintance, because of the highly emotional experiences we'd shared while finding a dead body and then working together to exonerate a wrongly accused suspect in the murder.

"I talked to Matt last night, and he said he'd be here first thing this morning," Stefan said. "He sounded a little tired. Sunny thought I'd woken him up. It was only 9:00, but he might have been jet-lagged and trying to adjust to local time."

The airports would have been clogged this week with people traveling for Thanksgiving. "He probably slept in this morning. Spending the holiday with family is fun, but it's also exhausting."

"He doesn't have any family," Stefan said absently. He looked past me and froze for a moment before saying, "Sorry, gotta get back to ironing."

He scurried away, and I turned to see Emma Quinn scowling at him. She might not yell at anyone, but she did give emphatic orders.

* * *

The air inside the museum was incredibly dry, making me wish I had a water bottle like the one I'd seen clipped to the male quilter's belt. I hurried over to the refreshment table to grab a couple of sugar cookies and look for something to drink. A sign next to the slow cooker announced that the mulled cider had been donated by a local farm, Pear Stirpes Orchard. I ladled out half a cup of the cider. I was in too much of a rush to drink it and burned my tongue, but at least it washed away the dryness, and the snack calmed the growling of my stomach.

At the other end of the table, the quilt instructor's assistant was talking nonstop in the shrillest voice I'd ever heard. Her words were addressed to Matt, who was listening politely. He looked in my direction, and I thought his eyes lit up with genuine interest, but I wasn't going to fall for his charm again. He was probably just hoping I'd rescue him from the assistant, and he would have been happy to see anyone who might rescue him from her.

I wasn't a naturally vengeful person, but it did feel good to leave Matt to her shrill mercies. Back at my appraisal station, one of the women who'd been waiting there earlier had disappeared, leaving only four women with quilts for me to look at.

Trudy rushed up to the desk, slightly out of breath. "I'm sorry. Meg's assistant caught me when I was in the bathroom, and she sent me out to the parking lot to get six boxes of supplies from her car, and I tried to explain that you needed me, but she didn't care."

"No problem," I said. "I just got back here myself, and I can handle the few remaining appraisals without your help. Why don't you go see if Emma has another project for you? And tell her how much I appreciated your help this morning."

Trudy left, and I finished the next two appraisals quickly, since the quilts had only recently been completed by the people who brought them in, so I didn't need to come up with a date for when they were made, and they were fairly common designs that didn't require me to look them up in my reference books. That left just two more quilts to appraise. They were owned by sisters in their sixties, who asked to have their appraisals done together. They'd brought in a pair of almost identical quilts. They'd designed them together, chosen the fabrics together, and then one sister did all the piecing for both quilts, and the other did all the appliqué. Once the tops had been completed, they'd each finished one, choosing different backings and making slightly different choices with their machine quilting so they could tell the two quilts apart.

The current value wasn't anywhere near what it should have been for all the work the women had put into the quilts, but they were definitely worth insuring. I advised them to get a more complete appraisal and also encouraged them to participate in the museum's registry of locally made quilts. Once they filled out the form, I made a little note at the bottom for Gil to keep in touch with the sisters in case they ever wanted to sell the quilts. Someday, if the quilts were kept together in good condition and with clear provenance, they might be a nice addition to the museum's collection. Linked quilts like these, where the provenance was established definitively, were extremely rare.

The women left happy, and I was able to pack up my supplies in my messenger bag. I kept out the registry forms for Gil, who had returned to the boardroom, but was deep in a conversation with a quilter I didn't recognize. I took the papers with me and headed over to the refreshment table for another cup of the mulled cider, which I hadn't had time to appreciate fully before.

While I waited for the cider to cool to drinking temperature, I watched the quilt teacher, Meg McLaughlin, return from yet another trip to the bathroom. She resumed making her rounds of the room, inspecting the work of each person at a sewing machine. Judging by the deepening frown on what seemed to be a naturally cheerful face, she must have found the finished pieces to be defective.

Meg walked over to the white board in the front of the room. Her shrill-voiced assistant, a woman as tall as Gil, but leaner and blonder, wearing ironed jeans and a green cashmere sweater, appeared at the teacher's side and clapped her hands. "Attention, everyone. Meg needs to talk to you."

Gil had been humming along to a traditional carol, but she stopped, leaving Peter, Paul, and Mary to carry on without her. The roar of the sewing machine motors and the background chatter faded.

"Thank you, Jayne." Meg adjusted her Santa hat. "I just wanted to make sure all the newcomers know that we have a diagram up here to follow."

Meg walked over to the nearest row of sewing machines, where the denim-clad man sat at one end. The service dog beside him stood and walked around to the front of the table, creating a barrier between the man and Meg. It wasn't hostile, exactly, but it was definitely anxious. Maybe it had something to do with the large pair of yellow-handled scissors that Meg had pulled out of the pocket of her pinafore apron.

Ignoring the dog, Meg reached over the table to snip off a completed block from the chain of them that draped over the back of the male quilter's sewing machine. She dropped the scissors back into her apron, held the block by two opposite edges, stretching it slightly, and then raised it to show everyone the side with all the seams. "Don't forget that for miniature blocks, it's absolutely critical that your seams be a scant quarter inch. There's just no room for error. Carl here has done an excellent job with his piecing. Everyone should look to him for inspiration."

The man flushed as if he'd just been criticized instead of praised. He pushed his seat back abruptly, stood, and snapped his fingers for the dog to follow him, which it did without hesitation. They both stomped out of the room.

Meg laughed and said, "Some men just can't take a compliment. Right, ladies?"

Meg's assistant led a chorus of agreement, and then Meg said, "Back to work now. No time to lose if we're going to finish enough ornaments for the museum to have a truly spectacular tree."

The sewing machines immediately roared into action, and Gil started humming along with "I'll Be Home for Christmas."

I decided to take that as my cue to head on home after a brief detour to hand off the registry forms to Gil.

CHAPTER THREE

———

"Dee sent me over to get you," Emma said before I'd taken a single step in Gil's direction. "She wants to make sure you're enjoying yourself."

There was no denying Emma or Dee, not that I wanted to. I liked them, and I could spare a few minutes before I went home. I finished the last of my cider and tossed my cup into the trash before following Emma back to the last of the long tables topped with sewing machines.

Physically, Dee Madison looked like the stereotype of a quilter: ancient, white haired, and a little stooped. Her businesslike red jacket and skirt messed with the expected image a bit, and anyone who'd spent more than five minutes with her knew she was more like a ruthless entrepreneur than a cuddly grandmother. A few months ago, when Dee had been frustrated by the lack of legal methods to shut down the seller of fake antique quilts, she'd proposed hiring a hit man to take care of the problem, and it hadn't been entirely clear to me that she was joking.

With her friends though, Dee was kind and generous. She patted the seat at the sewing machine next to her. "I saved you a spot."

"Someone who can actually sew should sit there." I remembered only too clearly my one and only experience in a sewing class, which had involved making a simple apron with just two large pieces of fabric, and I'd still managed to make a mess of it. In the wake of Meg's little lecture about precise seams, I wasn't about to try making miniature blocks made out of tiny bits of fabric that needed to be joined with absolute precision.

"These ornaments are so easy a child could make them," Dee said. "The Friendship Star block is particularly good for beginners."

I was familiar with the traditional block, at least in its completed form. It was a nine-patch variation, three rows of three squares each, some of the squares divided diagonally into two triangles of contrasting colors. Keeping with the holiday theme for today's blocks, the middle square was a red print, a red triangle butted up against each side of the center square, and then the four outer corners of the block were a white print. When everything was sewn together, the pieces formed a four-pointed star that looked a bit like a spinning pinwheel. It was a simple block, certainly, but still beyond my sewing skills

"Here," Dee said, picking up a pile of squares that were next to her sewing machine and placing them to the left of the machine she'd assigned me to. "I've already sewn the pairs of triangles into squares. All you have to do is sew the pieces into three rows. It's easy. Emma will iron them for you, and then you can sew the rows together, and you'll have made your very first quilt block."

Dee lined up a white square, another square made up of a red triangle and a white triangle, and then another white square. "Just sew them together in that order."

They were so tiny. Just one-and-a-half-inch square, including the seam allowances. I couldn't imagine how Dee had managed to join the tiny triangles into such a perfect square, and from what I'd heard the instructor say, anything less than perfection was a disaster. "I'm afraid I'll waste all the hard work that's already gone into them."

"Don't worry about it," Dee said. "It's not like someone will die if you mess it up. You can always rip out the seam and do it again. Go ahead and try it."

I glanced at Emma, knowing before I did that she would support whatever Dee wanted, so I wasn't surprised when I got a nod of encouragement in response. I turned back to the sewing machine. In theory, I knew how it worked from my one and only sewing class. But that was a long time ago, before I'd started passing out at the least little bit of stress. I didn't like to think about what could happen to fingers that weren't controlled by a conscious brain and drifted too near the speeding needle.

When I didn't immediately start sewing, Dee said, "You can watch me do a seam first, if you want. Just pick up the first two pieces. Align the two edges like this, and place them on the feed dogs so the needle will be a quarter inch from the raw edge. Drop the foot to hold them in place. Do a few backstitches, and then zoom on down to the other end before doing another bit of backstitching."

Dee demonstrated as she spoke, barely even looking at her hands. When she got to the zooming part, she stomped on the foot pedal like she was the little old lady from Pasadena who couldn't keep her foot off the accelerator.

"Isn't she a beaut?" Emma said from behind us. "It's a semi-industrial machine. Does up to fifteen hundred stitches per minute, about twice what the average home machine does. I don't know if you've met Sunny Kunik yet. She let us borrow the machines from her shop for the day, and now I don't want to go back to my own more basic model at home. I might have to ask Santa to bring me one just like this for Christmas. And I'm definitely getting a pair of Sunny's scissors for someone's stocking."

I picked up the first two pieces the way Dee did and managed to get them under the presser foot. "Are you sure I won't ruin anything?"

"I'm sure," Dee said. "Go ahead and step on the pedal."

My foot hovered. "But what about the seam allowance? How do I know it's right? I just heard Meg saying how important it was, but I didn't get a chance to go look at the sample she said was done so well."

"Don't worry about that," Dee said. "You'll never be as good as Carl Quincy, but that's okay."

Seizing on that as an excuse to avoid demonstrating my incompetence and ruining the pretty little triangles, I said, "Is that the man in denim who stomped out of here? Why was he so upset anyway?"

Dee sighed. "Meg had no way of knowing, but I wish she hadn't chosen Carl's work as an example. He's terribly conflicted about his quilting. It's not a macho enough hobby, you d he's terrified his friends on the police force will find out about it."

Emma reached down to realign the pieces under my sewing machine's presser foot. "Dee's been teaching him in private, and we've been trying to get him to come out of the quilting closet, because he really is quite talented. The other guild members could learn so much from him. And vice versa."

"But no," Dee said, shaking her head. "He's an ex-cop, you know. Retired on disability, and he hasn't come to grips with that either, so the idea of his friends knowing he enjoys what he still considers to be a hobby for little old ladies and invalids just makes it that much more difficult. It's such a pity. He loves quilting, and it's helped him cope with his anxiety over being retired, but doing it in public is another matter altogether."

"I was surprised he showed up today, even if it's a pretty safe bet none of his buddies from the force will be here," Emma said, making yet another infinitesimally small adjustment in the placement of the pieces on my sewing machine. "And now I'm not sure he'll ever come to another guild event. What a waste."

"He does really intricate work with near record-setting numbers of tiny pieces in each quilt," Dee said, "so it's not surprising Meg singled him out for his precision. I'm sure she thought he'd be pleased."

Emma reached down to adjust my fabric squares yet again. At this rate, they were going to be frayed to nothing but threads from all the friction against the feed dogs.

I slid out of the seat and stood up. "Why don't we switch places, Emma? You do the stitching, and I'll take the finished pieces to do the ironing. I think that's more my speed anyway. Unless you've got turbo-charged irons too?"

* * *

I carried the quilt pieces over to the ironing board where Stefan had been working, but he wasn't anywhere in the room that I could see. Neither was Meg McLaughlin, who was supposed to be in charge of helping beginners like myself. Even Gil was missing again, although I wasn't sure she knew any more about ironing than I did.

At least the iron didn't appear to be any different from the standard models I'd used before. What stumped me though was what exactly I was supposed to be doing with the three little rows of joined red-and-white fabrics. They weren't exactly wrinkled, so why was I ironing them?

I placed the three rows of the Friendship Star block on the ironing board and picked up the iron. I ran it over the surface of the board to confirm that it was working, and steam swirled up from the base plate. That much I knew how to do. Now what?

My uncertainty must have been obvious, because Meg's assistant came rushing over. She snapped, in her painfully shrill voice, "If you don't know what you're doing, you need to ask someone for instructions."

My pulse spiked as I fought the urge to snap right back at her. I took a calming breath and reminded myself that passing out with an iron in my hand wasn't any safer than losing consciousness with my fingers near the sewing machine's needle. "Okay. Can you help me?"

"Of course." The words were encouraging, but the shrill tone made them sound like an accusation. She took the iron out of my hand and set it down at the wide end of the ironing board. "I'm Jayne Connors. I always assist whenever Meg McLaughlin comes to Danger Cove. She taught me everything I know about quilting."

"Does she give classes in ironing too?"

Jayne didn't respond, but instead took the top row of the block and laid it upside down between us. She pointed at the seam allowances. "They all need to get pushed to one side of the seam, not spread apart like you'd do if you were making clothes." She turned the row over, right side up, and smoothed the seam allowances with her fingers before dropping the iron on the fabric. "Press it carefully until it's flat, making sure not to stretch the pieces out of shape."

Jayne raised the iron to reveal that the row, which had been a puffy blob from the bulk of the seams, was now a perfectly flat rectangle.

It seemed simple enough, but I still wasn't sure I could make the remaining pieces look so perfect. "What if they're not all nice and straight when I'm done?"

"Then you take them back to the sewing machine, rip out the seam, and sew it again until you get it right."

I didn't bother to explain that I hadn't done the sewing. I trusted Dee to have done an acceptable stitching job, so if the finished row wasn't straight, it was more likely due to my ironing than to her stitching. I took the second row, placed it in front of me right side up, did my best to push the seam allowances all to one side, and then reached for the iron.

"No, no, no." Jayne's voice was even sharper than before as she reclaimed the iron. "The seam allowances need to alternate from row to row." Jayne flipped the direction of the two seams, ironed them, and then placed the second row next to the first one she'd ironed so I could see which way the seams fell when the rows butted up against each other.

"Always have a plan for the ironing of the whole block before you start. You want to push the seam allowances toward the darker fabrics whenever possible, but also make sure that they're not both going in the same direction where two rows meet. Then, when the rows are put together, the extra layers alternate, and they don't form a big lump on one side."

While she spoke, she ironed the third row for me, pushing the seams in the right direction without any apparent thought, leaving nothing for me to do, which was probably just as well.

"I never realized how complicated ironing could be."

"Ironing can make or break a quilt," Jayne said. "Meg taught me that. Have you met her yet? She designed the ornaments we're making today."

"I've seen her in passing, but we didn't get formally introduced," I said. "She was in a bit of a hurry at the time."

"You'll love her," Jayne said. "She's easy to talk to, even now that she's famous. I always think of her as Mrs. Claus, even without the hat she's wearing today. Her husband doesn't look anything like Santa, which ruins the image, but he doesn't usually travel with her, so that's okay."

Meg did indeed look like every illustration I'd ever seen of Mrs. Claus: plump, rosy-cheeked, with white hair pulled up into a loose bun, and wearing little round spectacles. The Santa hat and the red-and-white pinafore-style apron that she wore with black pants only added to the impression. Jayne, on the other hand, looked like an oversized elf in her green sweater. A mean elf, gleefully placing lumps of coal in bad kids' stockings.

"Oh no," Jayne said, peering at something on the other side of the room. "That woman is doing it again. I thought Meg was going to talk to her, but it looks like she didn't have a chance. I'd better go deal with it."

"Don't let me stop you." I had no idea what quilting crime was happening on the other side of the room or how Jayne had spotted it. Still, if it meant that I would get off with just a warning from the quilt police, I had to be grateful that someone else was doing something worse than I was.

* * *

I abandoned my short-lived post at the ironing board and carried the ironed pieces back to Emma and Dee. I felt like a fraud, since Jayne had done all the work.

Matt Viera had joined Dee and Emma while I was learning just how much of a science ironing could be. He was perched on the very corner of the table where Dee was seated. As I approached, a woman in her fifties, wearing a quilted red-and-white vest, came over from the refreshments table. "Excuse me, Matteo," she said in a breathless voice. When he turned to look at who was calling him, she waved her phone at him. "May I?"

"Sure." He slid around to the end of the table and held out his arm so she could snuggle in beside him.

She held her phone out, took several selfies, and checked to make sure the images were acceptable before saying, "Thank you. I told my Facebook friends that I'd met you at another quilting event, but they kept saying that without a picture, it didn't happen. Now I've got the proof."

When had arts reporters become such celebrities that people would ask to take pictures with them? Even male fashion models weren't widely known by name, so why would this woman have been bragging about meeting him to her Facebook friends? Or was it just because he was an incredibly good-looking man, even when he wasn't painstakingly cleaned up, dressed and polished for the camera?

Actually, now that I thought about it, I could have sworn that Matt had grown even better looking since I last saw him three months ago. Absence truly did make the heart grow fonder.

The selfie-taker wandered off happily, and Matt turned back to face me and Dee. "Keely, it's good to finally see you again."

For a moment, I was distracted by the perfect planes of his face and the look in his dark eyes that suggested seeing me again had made his day. Then I remembered the last three months of silence from him. He had my number, and he knew where I lived. If he'd wanted to see me that badly, there hadn't been anything to stop him. I'd believed he was interested in me before, and I'd been wrong. I wasn't going to make that mistake again. This time, I knew there was nothing personal in his attention to me, any more than there had been in his gracious willingness to be in the woman's selfies. His nice-guy persona was just part of his skills as a reporter.

"Nice to see you too," I said politely, but without any warmth. Forewarned was forearmed, and I'd made a whole career out of being prepared to resist any sort of emotional manipulation during negotiations. The only thing I didn't understand was why Matt was even bothering to work his magic on me today. Back in August, he'd needed my help to get the scoop on who had killed Randall Tremain, but there was nothing truly newsworthy about today's event. "You must be here to write about the start of a new holiday tradition at the museum."

"Among other things." He swung one leg back and forth a few inches, drawing my attention to the ridiculous pockets on his thigh and the strong muscles beneath the cotton fabric. "Have they converted you yet?"

"To quilting?" I tossed the ironed rows onto the table next to Dee's sewing machine. "No. I'm only qualified to fetch and carry. I can't even iron properly, apparently. What about you? When are you going to take up quilting?"

"I can sew already. I'm planning to make a couple of the ornaments today. I just wanted to say hi to my favorite quilters first."

Dee's machine stopped. "If you sign the ornaments you make, I bet Gil could auction them off for a fortune after the tree comes down."

He shook his head ever so slightly at Dee and then looked at me again. "Hey, I just remembered. You still owe me a tour of the bank vault in your home. I'll call you next week to set it up."

I knew he didn't mean it, and still I almost believed he'd call this time.

Before I could respond, I was distracted by a commotion over near the refreshments table. Jayne Connors's shrill voice had gotten even louder and harder to ignore. She was shrieking at poor Trudy Kline, making me regret not paying more attention to who had distracted Jayne from lecturing me. Of all the people in the room, Trudy was the least capable of standing up for herself.

Despite Jayne's angry, piercing tone, I only caught about half of the words, something about washing hands *thoroughly* before returning to the cutting table after eating and the damage that a little bit of grease or chocolate could do to fabric.

Meg McLaughlin came in from yet another trip to the ladies' room just in time to intervene. Living up to her cuddly Mrs. Claus appearance, Meg drew her protégée out into the hallway to cool down, leaving the red-faced Trudy to be surrounded and reassured by other members of the quilt guild. The women seemed to know what would cheer her up, which mostly consisted of talking about her charm bracelet, judging from the way they bent over it and admired it. Trudy preened under their attention, like a recently engaged woman showing off an engagement ring.

Dee sighed. "We have to do something about Jayne. Emma, please make sure to add it to the agenda for our next board meeting. It can go under old business."

"Ancient business." Emma seemed to realize Matt and I didn't know what they were talking about, and she explained. "This isn't the first time she's caused a scene at a guild event. She's a total control freak, and she gets confrontational when things don't go according to her plan. Shouting is only the first stage. She's been known to throw things if she doesn't feel she's being listened to. She stabbed a table with a pair of scissors once when we were working on a quilt for a fundraiser. Fortunately, it wasn't one of Sunny's heavy-duty scissors, or it would have caused a lot more damage."

"Why haven't you banned Jayne from membership if she's that much trouble?"

"We may have to," Dee said. "I'd rather convince her to see a therapist or something. She's really an extraordinary needlewoman, and her quilts are popular at our shows. She won the Best of Show ribbon about five years ago, and she probably deserved it every year since. The quilts are judged without names attached, but I think the judges recognized her style and let their personal dislike sway their votes. They couldn't deny her a blue ribbon, because her quilts are stunning, but they could pass her over for the very top award."

"Still," I said, "it sounds like she could be dangerous. To the guild's property and maybe even to other members."

"It's complicated," Emma said. "It's not just that she's a really good quilter, but she's also close with Meg McLaughlin, and no one's sure how Meg would react if we kicked her friend out of the guild. Meg's the most famous quilter ever to come from Danger Cove, and she teaches all around the world. She lives in Seattle now, but she was originally from here, and she's good about remembering where she came from. She turns down other events if they conflict with our show so she can be here. Her presence at our show brings in a lot of paying visitors who wouldn't come otherwise. Plus, she does one workshop a year for the guild without charge. That's why she's here today and why we have so many volunteers. Your appraisals brought in people too, and some of our guild members would have come just to help out the museum, but most are only here so they can meet Meg and learn from her."

Trudy had recovered her composure and was over at the fabric-cutting table near the entrance, laughing with a couple of other guild members. They'd hastily braided a simple red-and-white crown out of some fabric strips too narrow to use and bestowed it on her, dubbing her a quilting princess for the day.

Jayne and Meg hadn't returned, and I hoped that Meg had been able to convince Jayne that she'd helped more than enough for the day and should go home.

I still needed to find Gil and give her the papers for the quilt registry. She must have left again while I'd been learning about ironing. She definitely wasn't here now, and if she'd been here when the incident between Jayne and Trudy started, Gil would have kept it from escalating to an uncomfortable situation.

I couldn't go home until I'd handed off the paperwork, but if I didn't get away from Dee and Emma right now, I was going to get roped into operating one of the dangerous weapons that masqueraded as harmless sewing machines. "I'm starved. I think I'll go see if there's anything left at the refreshment table."

"I'll come with you." Matt straightened and ambled across the room with me.

"Stefan was looking for you a few minutes ago. Did he catch you?"

Matt shook his head. "I haven't seen him yet."

I turned to look at the ironing station where I'd seen Stefan earlier, but he still hadn't returned. "He can't have gone far. I doubt he'd leave before he got the chance to introduce you to his girlfriend. They were hoping you'd interview her about her quilt shop's contributions to today's event."

"What did you think of Sunny? Is she as perfect as Stefan says?"

"Sunny seems to be everything that Stefan has ever claimed about her, even the traits that seemed too good to be true." I surveyed the remnants of the refreshments on the conference table. There wasn't even a crumb large enough to tempt a night-before Christmas mouse to stir. "She's obviously devoted to him, and she's lovely, smart, and strong minded."

"I suppose that means that now both of them will be picking on me for my failure to live up to their expectations?"

"From what I've seen, Sunny might *think* that you're a disappointment, but unlike Stefan, she knows better than to say it out loud."

"Where is she?" Matt said. "I do want to meet her and talk about her shop, but I can't stay for long today."

"A reporter's work is never done?"

"That too," Matt said. "But I've got a meeting with some business associates at the Smugglers' Tavern this afternoon."

Business associates, not fellow reporters. That was odd. None of my business, and I wasn't going to ask.

"Sunny had to go get some supplies at her quilt shop," I said. "She should be back any minute now though. It shouldn't take much more than half an hour to pop over there, get what she needs, and drive back here. It's been at least that long since she left. In fact, that's probably why Stefan isn't here right now. He probably went outside to help her unload her car."

"I'll give them another half hour, just in case she got tied up with an emergency at the shop," Matt said. "It'll give me a chance to make an ornament or two, but then I really need to leave. I can meet Sunny at her shop some other time."

I was lifting the lid on the slow cooker to see if there was any mulled cider left, when screams from outside startled me into dropping it back in place. The room's windows were above eye level, so we couldn't see outside, but even if we could have, the sounds seemed to be coming from the direction of the back parking lot. Someone must have left the back door propped open so the quilters would have easy access to the upstairs boardroom without trekking through the rest of the museum.

Matt and I looked at each other for a moment, and I assumed that, like me, he was remembering the last time we'd been together and heard a woman screaming—the day Randall Tremain's body had been found by his business partner. Just like then, Matt came to his senses before I did and raced out of the boardroom and down the back stairs with me at his heels.

We followed the screams out through the museum's employee-only back door, which had indeed been propped open for today's event. There was a loading dock about halfway down the back of the building, and then beyond it a fenced-in area jutted out into the parking lot to contain the museum's Dumpsters. Sunny Kunik was at the far corner of the fencing, with her back to me and Matt, still screaming hysterically.

It wasn't obvious what the problem was until we stumbled to a stop beside her. There, on the ground just past the trash enclosure, was the bloody and apparently lifeless body of Alan Miller.

CHAPTER FOUR

———

Sunny's screams tapered off. I took her by the shoulders, turned her around, and walked her over to a picnic table that had been set up for museum employees to take breaks during nice weather. It was directly across from the back door of the museum and far enough away from the trash enclosure that we couldn't see the body any longer. Matt called 9-1-1 and then apparently noticed that curious quilters were emerging from the museum to see what was happening. He went over to encourage everyone to remain huddled there, a safe distance from the crime scene.

Stefan pushed his way through the crowd to rush over to the picnic table. He took Sunny in his arms.

"Shock," Sunny said, her voice trembling. "Need to lie down. Raise feet."

I heard sirens in the distance. Help was on its way for Sunny, even if it was too late for Alan.

Gil appeared beside me, as calm and confident as ever. "You can use my office, Sunny. There's a sofa in there where you can lie down. I'll stay here to let the police know where you are. Help yourself to some water from the mini fridge."

"No," Sunny said, extricating herself from Stefan so she could sit sideways on the picnic table bench. She lay down and closed her eyes. "Can't move. And nothing to drink until paramedics check me out."

"She's got medical training," Stefan said as he knelt beside the picnic table bench. "It's always best to do what she says."

Matt called out my name from where he stood at the back door. He tossed me his truck's keys. "Look in the duffel bag behind the driver's side seat. It's got a blanket for emergencies."

"I'll be right back," I told Stefan before hurrying off to get the blanket. I recognized Matt's battered old truck immediately. I'd ridden in it once, back when I'd thought he was an impoverished reporter, but I'd later learned that he could easily have paid cash for any vehicle he wanted, up to and including the most expensive luxury models. And this beat-up clunker was what he'd chosen.

I didn't have time to dwell on his quirks at the moment. I unlocked the driver's door, and right where Matt had said to look, I found a synthetic fleece blanket. I grabbed it and headed back to the picnic table. I could hear Stefan making soft, reassuring sounds, although I couldn't tell if they were actually words.

I didn't want to startle them, so I whispered, "I've got the blanket."

Stefan took it from me and wrapped it around Sunny. The sound of sirens grew louder, and Matt sent Trudy out to Main Street to flag down the first responders and point them to the back of the museum.

Feeling helpless and useless, I was surprised to not also feel lightheaded and nauseated. Apparently the adrenaline from seeing poor Alan's body had counteracted any inclination my nervous system might have had to send me into unconsciousness. Too bad I couldn't carry around a shot of adrenaline like people with severe allergies carried an EpiPen, for when I started to feel the symptoms of a syncope event.

Two patrol cops I'd met before, the veteran Fred Fields and rookie Richie Faria, were the first to come running down the driveway. Matt pointed them in the direction of the body. A few seconds later, a pair of paramedics arrived to follow in the cops' footsteps. A second set of paramedics arrived moments later, and Matt sent them over to check on Sunny.

The paramedics politely but firmly moved Stefan out of their way, leaving him looking as helpless as I felt. He tugged at his bow tie.

"She could have been killed." Stefan stood next to me, keeping his gaze fixed on his girlfriend. "If she'd arrived in the parking lot just a few minutes sooner, she could have been killed."

"It doesn't do any good to dwell on what might have happened." At least that was what I'd always told my clients. Putting the advice into practice myself was another matter. I'd never managed to actually let go of that type of second-guessing of my behavior, especially when it came to whether I could have done a better job for my clients. "Sunny's safe now."

"We don't know that," Stefan said. "She wouldn't say whether she'd been injured. What if she was shot and just hasn't felt it yet because she's in so much shock?"

"I didn't hear a gun, and I didn't see any blood on her. Did you?"

He squinted at Sunny through his little round glasses. "I didn't think to look. I'm such an idiot. And now she's covered with a blanket, so I can't see anything."

"The paramedics are with her, and they'll check her out."

"But she could have died," Stefan wailed. "And I haven't even told her how much I love her and that I want to spend the rest of my life with her. It would be such a cliché if she died without knowing, and she hates clichés. She'd never forgive me."

"She's not going to die," I said, reasonably sure there was nothing wrong with Sunny that some time and emotional support wouldn't fix.

"The museum should have had better security." He turned to glare at Gil.

"It's the middle of the day, just a few feet from Main Street in quiet little Danger Cove," I said. "It's not like we're in some gang-infested, drug-dealing, big-city slum."

"Maybe not, but it's awfully isolated back here. Nobody can see what's going on from the street or any of the adjoining buildings."

He was right about that much. The driveway was nothing more than a narrow alley, which had been more than adequate when the building had been constructed in 1898, but was barely wide enough for today's massive SUVs. On the opposite side of the building, an eight-foot-high solid plank fence ran from the back corner of the building, along a side street to the far corner of the property, and then across the other two sides of the parking lot and driveway, all the way around to Main Street.

It wasn't entirely private back here though. I pointed at the two security cameras, one on each corner of the building. "There are at least two witnesses. They can see everything that happens back here."

"The cameras couldn't stop what happened though." Stefan covered his face with his hands. One of his neatly turned-back sleeves had unfolded and was flapping loose. "I should have gone with Sunny instead of letting her go to the shop all by herself. It's my fault that she was alone and in danger."

"I just met Sunny, but I don't think she'd appreciate your hovering over her like that."

"But she could have died," Stefan repeated with every bit as much distraught emotion as the first time.

Right. Much as I preferred an appeal to logic, it wasn't going to have any effect on him right now. Perhaps an emotional approach would work better. "You can't fall apart on her now. She's going to need you. You have to be strong so you can support her when the paramedics declare her to be okay. Can you do that?"

He peered out from behind his hands and nodded uncertainly. "I can do anything that will help Sunny."

The paramedics, who'd been crouched beside Sunny, rose to their feet and looked around. One of them caught sight of Stefan and apparently recognized him as the person who'd been holding the hand of the patient when they'd arrived. He gestured for Stefan to return to her side.

"Go on," I said. "It doesn't look like they're going to insist on taking her to the hospital."

Stefan hurried over to be with Sunny. The one good thing about his panic over her safety was that it had prevented him from thinking about another, more likely risk: that the police would think Sunny was the one who'd killed Alan Miller. She would definitely be a suspect, since she'd found the body. She didn't have any apparent motive, however, so I wasn't particularly concerned. Besides, the museum's cameras had undoubtedly captured the entire crime, and Sunny would be ruled out as soon as the police viewed the videos.

Unless, of course, Sunny had actually killed Alan.

*   *   *

I returned to the steps outside the back door of the museum. Carl Quincy, apparently acting on instincts drilled into him during his years as a cop, had taken charge of the quilters and herded them back inside the museum to wait in the hallway until the detective in charge of the case arrived.

Matt remained outside on the back steps with me and Gil. We couldn't see Alan's body from there, just occasional glimpses of a paramedic or one of the responding cops if they stepped out from the cover of the trash enclosure.

We had a better view of the picnic table where the paramedics appeared to have declared Sunny to be out of danger. They were packing up their supplies and letting Stefan kneel beside her, holding her hand again.

Gil headed over to collect Sunny and Stefan so they could wait for the homicide detective in her office. She'd just gotten them inside the museum's back door when Officer Fred Fields stepped back from the crime scene and pointed toward me and Matt. Beside him was an older man in a suit. I hadn't seen him arrive, but I recognized him as the detective who'd been in charge of the Randall Tremain investigation a few months ago.

Bud Ohlsen was a large man, tall and not exactly fat, but his solid build had softened as he neared retirement age. His eyes remained sharp despite the wrinkles around them. He stared at the ground as he walked over to us and stopped a couple of feet from the back steps. I knew from past experience that there was no point in saying anything until Ohlsen had finished whatever train of thought he was following. When he'd interviewed me in the aftermath of Randall Tremain's murder, I'd initially thought the prolonged silences were an affectation, a conscious effort to guilt witnesses into filling the silence by spilling all their secrets. I'd since come to believe it was just a habit he'd developed over his long career, blocking out distractions while he focused on whatever little piece of evidence he was considering.

While he thought, I considered what information I might have to offer him. I'd been in the boardroom all morning without leaving for any reason until Sunny screamed. I was pretty sure the same was true for Dee and Emma. I knew they had definitely been in the boardroom between the time Alan Miller left to wait for his ride and the first of Sunny's screams. I'd been with them for part of that time, resisting their efforts to convert me into a quilter. Matt had been there throughout that same time frame too, arriving just as Alan left and then working the room for his job, interviewing Meg McLaughlin and then getting stuck listening to Jayne Conners.

Unfortunately, I couldn't vouch for the whereabouts of anyone else. Stefan and Gil had both been in and out of the boardroom all morning. So had Meg McLaughlin, with her constant trips to the ladies' room. Jayne had been out of sight for a bit while she was in time-out for yelling at Trudy. Trudy had made some trips out to the parking lot in that time frame, but I couldn't imagine someone as meek as she was committing murder. Carl Quincy had definitely been outside the boardroom for a while, having stomped out after he'd been praised by Meg, and I hadn't noticed when he and his dog had returned. Elizabeth Ashby had left at the same time as Alan, apparently on her way home, since she'd never come back inside. The rest of the quilters I didn't know well enough to have noticed if they'd left the room.

Detective Ohlsen reached the end of his train of thought and looked up to assess his two waiting witnesses.

"We've got to stop meeting like this," he said. "And if that's not possible, I expect you both to mind your own business and let me do my job."

"Of course," I said.

Ohlsen frowned at Matt. "And you, I expect you to not compromise my investigation. Don't even think of quoting me unless I specifically say my words are on the record."

"Hey," Matt said with a shrug. "I'm just an arts reporter. Nothing to do with criminal stuff."

Ohlsen snorted, obviously recalling the front-page story Matt had written about the capture of Randall Tremain's killer.

"I'm serious. After you two give your statement, you need to stay out of the investigation."

"Just tell me one thing," I said. "Alan is dead, right?"

Ohlsen nodded. "Stabbed several times. Which, if you need a reason to do what I tell you, is why you should stay out of it. Whoever killed him is strong and angry and vicious. If you start meddling, he could come after you next."

"Strong? As in, capable of moving him after he was killed?" Even as I spoke, I realized something had been bothering me about the crime scene. What had Alan been doing way over beyond the trash enclosure? "He was waiting for a friend, and I would have expected him to be out on Main Street, not back here. It would have been quicker and easier for his friend to pick him up out there, without having to drive down the narrow little alley."

"We don't know for sure that he was waiting for a ride," Ohlsen said, "He could have lied to you. It's possible he was actually casing the museum to steal from it. The victim fell into the category that you're going to end up in soon: *well known to the police*. It's not a good label to have. Trust me. And stay out of this."

Ohlsen was a good detective, and he'd find out soon enough that Alan Miller hadn't needed to loiter in the parking lot to check out the museum. He'd had free run of the building while getting his grandmother's quilt appraised. If Ohlsen didn't figure that out on his own, I'd explain it when my formal statement was taken. Assuming that was even necessary. With a little luck, the video cameras would show exactly what had happened, and the police wouldn't need anything from me.

Of course, luck didn't seem to be with me today. Otherwise, everyone would have had a wonderful time making ornaments, there wouldn't have been any tears, and no one would have been hurt, let alone killed.

CHAPTER FIVE

———

Matt didn't seem particularly upset about being sent away from the crime scene to wait with me and the other potential witnesses. His more hard-news colleagues would have been frantic, wanting to get the scoop, but he didn't even look back over his shoulder as he went inside.

We walked up the stairs in silence, the reality of what had happened settling on me. We'd been having a mostly pleasant holiday event filled with the generosity and cheer of the season, until it had suddenly been overshadowed by death and the reminder that "peace on earth and goodwill toward men" was as much of an unachievable goal as my own pursuit of perfection.

At the top of the stairs, Matt continued on to the boardroom to the right, while I turned left. I passed the restroom and the employees' break room on the way to Gil's office suite to check on Stefan and Sunny.

Gil was in the outer waiting room, with her back to me, staring thoughtfully at her own private office's closed door.

"How are they?" I asked her.

She started and turned around. "As well as can be expected, I suppose."

"How about you? You look…" I was used to Gil being essentially unfazeable, capable of handling any emergency the museum or, more often, its board of directors threw at her. I'd only seen her this upset once before, back when she'd been wrongfully ousted from her job here. And she wasn't singing. That was never good. "You look frazzled."

She smiled sadly. "That's exactly how I feel. I keep thinking I should be doing something to fix the situation, but *how to deal with a murder at your workplace* was never on the syllabus in business school."

"Not at law school either," I said. "And it definitely wasn't part of the curriculum in my quilt appraisal training."

"I don't suppose it was. Everyone thinks quilters are sweet, cheerful souls whose only quirk is a harmless obsession with fabric and thread. They've obviously never seen quilters arguing with a judge at a show. Professional wrestlers could learn a lot from listening to competing quilters' trash talk."

"I'm sure the police will get everything sorted out quickly," I said. "I know Detective Bud Ohlsen, and he's good at what he does. As soon as he gets a look at the museum's security tapes, he'll have the case closed within a few hours."

Gil hummed a bit of "Blue Christmas" and then sighed. "I'm afraid it won't be that easy. Apparently some local kids have been competing to see how many security cameras they can knock out. They hit the museum a few days ago, and because it's happened everywhere in town this week, our security company has a backlog of work. The first appointment I could get to fix the cameras is next week. It shouldn't have been a big deal. We've never ever had any problems in the parking lot. The directors have even been complaining that the cameras are a waste of money, considering how safe Danger Cove is, especially here on Main Street. I guess that's one good thing that will come out of today's terrible events. I won't get any more hassles about the cameras. Except, of course, for being blamed for not fixing the broken ones fast enough."

"You just can't win, can you?"

She shook her head. "I'll worry about that later, once the scene's been cleared. For now, I need to concentrate on keeping everyone calm."

"They'll probably send a patrol cop or two upstairs to keep an eye on everyone," I said. "If it's Fred Fields, he's good with people. Richie Faria, not so much."

"Good to know," Gil said, pasting a determined smile on her face. "I'll take care of Faria if he becomes a problem. He can't be any harder to manage than my board members."

"I'll take on the really tricky job," I told her. "I'll make sure Dee doesn't provoke the cops."

* * *

From the doorway of the boardroom, I looked for Dee and Emma. They were still at their sewing machines, not stitching, but surrounded by quilt guild members looking to them for guidance. That could be a problem if Dee got some wild idea in her head.

I was about to go over and make good on my promise to Gil when I heard someone approaching from behind me. I turned to see the rookie officer, Richie Faria, coming to an abrupt stop to stare at me in surprise. He must not have noticed me earlier during his race to the crime scene.

We had met during the investigation of Randall Tremain's murder. Faria had only been on the Danger Cove police force for a year or two, but he was eager for advancement to the role of major crime detective, so he volunteered for any assignment that might give him that sort of experience. He was in his midtwenties, blond, and clean cut. He was also a few inches shorter than average, but with the kind of athletic build that world-class tennis players might envy. He bounced on the balls of his feet as he resumed walking toward me.

"Not you again." He held up his head. "No, don't tell me. I'm guessing you've solved the murder for us already, and we're just wasting our time following standard police procedure."

Faria had been quick to discount me the last time I'd dealt with him too, and apparently the fact that his skepticism had almost gotten me killed hadn't changed his attitude.

"I'm not any happier to be a witness to another death than you are to see me," I said. "We're both stuck here for the time being though."

"Just don't get any ideas about doing our jobs for us."

"Wouldn't dream of it," I lied. I'd never been any good at sitting back and waiting for others to take care of a problem. Matt's irreverent attitude must have rubbed off on me, because I couldn't help goading Faria a little. "I'll be here though, if you need any help."

He snorted and then glanced around the room, something he probably should have done before confronting me, to make sure there wasn't any trouble brewing. His gaze settled on Carl Quincy, who was seated at the first sewing machine table about ten feet from the entrance. His machine was turned off, and there were no quilt pieces on the table, just a few pins and a pair of Sunny's yellow-handled scissors. Carl was turned sideways in the seat, patting his dog and telling him he was a good boy.

Faria called over to Carl. "Hey, what are you doing here? You got a girlfriend now, and she dragged you along for the day?"

I could see the wheels turning in Carl's head. He hadn't been all that happy about his quilting skills being the center of attention earlier, even among the sympathetic women in the room, and he definitely wasn't ready to admit he enjoyed a traditionally female activity to someone who was sure to spread the news among all the members of the Danger Cove Police Department. Presumably, Carl didn't have a girlfriend, and he was constitutionally incapable of lying, or he'd have jumped on that explanation. I almost took pity on him, claiming myself as his girlfriend. I thought better of it though, since we were witnesses to a homicide, after all, and even a little white lie might come back to haunt both of us.

"None of your business," Carl finally managed in a gruff tone. "I don't owe rookies any explanation for where I go or who I'm with."

Faria shrugged. "Whatever. No need to get all huffy."

"Just do your job, officer."

Faria had already dismissed Carl from his thoughts and was headed over to where the more senior uniformed officer, Fred Fields, was at the conference table, staring sadly at the empty plates that had held an assortment of Christmas cookies earlier.

Dee and Emma were a safe distance from both officers, so I could take a minute or two to introduce myself to Carl. I went over to where he sat with his dog. "We haven't met. I'm Keely Fairchild. Not a quilter, but an appraiser. Dee and Emma have told me about what amazing work you do."

"Thanks." He blushed until he was almost the color of the Labradoodle.

"If you ever decide to get your quilts insured, they'll need to be appraised. I hope you'll give me a call. I'll get you a business card from my bag later, or you can ask Dee and Emma. They know how to reach me."

"I will."

"How's your dog coping with the chaos today?"

Carl's color was returning to normal, and he ruffled the dog's fur. "He's fine. He's a lot tougher than I am these days."

I could tell from Carl's tone just how frustrated he was at not being part of the action. I certainly knew the feeling. It didn't help that Faria had essentially just rubbed Carl's nose in the fact that he wasn't the powerful person he'd once been.

"You did a great job of getting the gawkers up here and keeping everyone calm. You made the responding officers' job a lot easier."

"Old habits die hard."

"You must have worked a lot of crime scenes over the course of your career," I said. "Perhaps you could tell me what's going to happen next. Starting with how soon we're going to be rid of Richie Faria."

Carl wrinkled his nose. "Not for quite a while. There are an awful lot of people to take statements from. The detective will want to create a timeline for what happened, and that means getting everyone's recollection, comparing the stories, then possibly going back and requestioning some of the witnesses if there are any discrepancies."

"Especially the ones who don't have alibis and could be the killer?"

"Mmm." He opened a pocket on the dog's vest and retrieved a biscuit. "They can't be sure it isn't one of us, so, yeah, they'll probably keep us all holed up here until they have at least a basic theory of the case."

"Even you?" I said.

"Especially me." Carl used hand gestures to have his dog sit, shake hands, and then lie down before handing over the treat. "I must have just missed the altercation between the victim and his killer. I didn't see anyone or hear anything unusual when I was out back, but I'd just come inside from walking Rusty, when the screams started. Bud Ohlsen's a thorough detective, and he won't give me any special treatment. He has to consider me a potential suspect since I don't have an alibi, and there were quite a few witnesses to my confrontation with the Miller kid this morning, which suggests I could have a motive."

"You were arguing, not getting physical."

"I'm not saying I killed the kid, just that, viewed objectively, I've got to be considered a suspect. Some of us—retired cops, I mean—never adjust to leaving the force, especially when it's for health reasons. Everyone knows I didn't want to retire, but between the diabetes and a spinal injury, I didn't trust myself to be able to back up a partner. Anyway, the joke is that old cops don't die, they just become security guards. But the real worry is that they become vigilantes."

"Why would a vigilante go after a kid like Alan Miller?"

"No reason I can see," Carl said. "I wasn't happy to see him here, because I'd rousted him more than a few times in the past. No juvie record, but he started acting out as soon as he graduated from high school. He's pretty well known to us, but we couldn't make anything stick. Nothing that was worth prosecuting anyway. Little stuff, mostly. Shoplifting, minor scuffles outside bars, that sort of thing. It could have just been that he hung out with a bad crowd. A few of his friends did end up doing some serious time while he skated free. Still, seeing him here, I was worried that he might make off with some of the tools that Sunny donated or perhaps something from the museum's archives down the hall."

The archives were secure behind passkeyed and alarmed doors, but Sunny's tools had been scattered everywhere in the boardroom. If Alan had stolen any of Sunny's donations, she might have noticed and confronted him about it in the parking lot. "Do you think he did take anything?"

"Not that I saw." Carl patted the dog thoughtfully. "Not even any of the refreshments, now that I think of it. Maybe he really was here for legitimate reasons."

"It'll be interesting to hear what the police found on his body."

"Anything he could fit in a pocket certainly wasn't worth dying for," Carl said, shaking his head. "Probably wasn't what got him killed either. More likely he was double-crossed by one of the hooligans he hangs out with. I should have escorted him out to the front sidewalk as soon as I recognized him."

"If you're right and he was killed by his supposed friends, getting him out of here wouldn't have changed anything."

"It might have," Carl said. "The least little thing can derail a crime. At least that's what we have to believe on the job, that we can make a difference by making it a little bit harder for the criminals. Sort of like the butterfly effect, where a tiny event in one corner of the planet can have huge effects halfway across the globe. If I'd handled Alan better, he might still be alive."

"No one can anticipate every possible consequence to his actions. There are too many variables. In fact, if Alan was killed by anyone other than the person coming to give him a ride, I might have been able to prevent it by insisting that Alan wait inside for his friend." I called on the tone of voice I'd once used to reassure nervous clients worried about taking the witness stand. "It wasn't your fault. You can't blame yourself."

Carl didn't seem any more convinced that he was free of responsibility for Alan's death than I was about my own lack of responsibility for the situation. I couldn't bring Alan back to life, but I could do my best to make sure the police found the person who had actually killed him.

CHAPTER SIX

———

Officer Faria was trotting around the room, confiscating all of Sunny's yellow-handled scissors from the various workstations, understandably uncomfortable being surrounded by all those sharp instruments in the aftermath of a stabbing. He was missing the real threat though. Apparently he hadn't figured out yet that the rotary cutters were like pizza cutters on steroids, with what amounted to circular razor blades in them, or he'd have collected them first.

Still, I was grateful that Faria's work took him away from Officer Fred Fields, so I could quiz him on what was going on outside without having to deal with Faria's condescension.

I knew Fred from the stress support group we both attended at the county hospital. He was about average height, and his uniform seemed to be a little bit tighter around the middle every time I saw him, since his favorite coping tool for stress was to indulge in sugary treats. Fred was in his mid-thirties, a seasoned officer, with no particular aspirations to rise through the ranks. He liked being on patrol where he felt like he was making a difference, stopping to chat with the local citizens. He took crimes personally, as if he alone were to blame for not having anticipated and prevented them, which led to his need for the stress support group meetings.

"I heard there were refreshments," he said. "Where are they?"

"Gone, I'm afraid." Seeing the look of disappointment on his face, I added, "You didn't miss much. Most of the treats had chocolate in them." That was about the only sugary food I'd ever seen him refuse, and if he was desperate enough, he'd eat a chocolate chip cookie and spit out the chips as if they were watermelon seeds.

He sighed. "I was hoping there might be some oatmeal-raisin cookies. Oatmeal's good for me. My wife's always making it for me."

Not in the form of cookies, I suspected, but all I said was, "How long do you think we'll be stuck here?"

"It could be a while," he said. "I'm under orders to make sure no one leaves until everyone's contact information has been collected, along with anything they might know about the incident. I'm going to need to take your phone, by the way. I've already collected everyone else's. No calls until you've given your statement. Unless you want to call a lawyer, of course, and then I'll make the arrangements."

I dug the phone out of my pocket and stared at it, reluctant to hand it over. It had taken me a long time to accept that I needed to have that kind of lifeline within reach at all times for medical reasons, but now that I had accepted this new reality, I found it nerve wracking to let go of the phone. Still, I didn't really need it as long as I was here at the museum, surrounded by cops who could summon help if I needed it.

I handed Fred the phone, and he dropped it into a plastic baggie. He wrote my name on the outside and then tucked it into the pocket of his uniform jacket. "I'll add it to the rest of the collection when I get a chance."

"Any idea what happened to Alan Miller?"

Fred narrowed his eyes, and his stiff posture radiated disapproval that a crime had taken place in *his* town. "All I know is that a young guy is dead. What a waste."

"I heard he had a record," I said. "Or not exactly a record, but he was 'well known to police.' Did you know him?"

"He wasn't that bad," he said. "Stupid stuff, nothing malicious. Just didn't think before he acted or spoke."

"I met him briefly this morning, and I was wondering if he might have been high on something."

"It's possible," Fred said. "And drugs can certainly make people do stupid things, ruin their lives before they get a chance to do anything."

"Or end their lives." It just seemed so wrong that a young man had been killed while trying to do something nice for his grandmother.

Fred nodded and stared desperately at the empty cookie plates, as if he might have overlooked something there that would help him cope with his distress.

My stomach grumbled, unmoved by the tragedy. "I know none of us can make any phone calls, but do you think you could call in a take-out lunch order for us? I'm starved, and I bet other people are too. Most of the people in the room have been here since before I arrived, and they've been working nonstop. We could get something for Carl's dog too, if he says it's okay."

"I think that could be arranged. If Ohlsen doesn't want anyone coming over here to deliver, I'll find someone to run across the street to the teriyaki place. You'll have to put together the order and arrange for payment though. Faria will rat me out if I get too involved. Not proper procedure, he'll say. Like he's got so much experience. I may not be as formally educated as he is, but I do know that hungry witnesses are not cooperative witnesses."

"Just give me a few minutes to find out what everyone wants." I was more than happy to pay for the lunch and collect everyone's order. I'd been planning a donation to the museum this month anyway, and keeping the volunteers fed would benefit everyone. Besides, collecting the orders would give me an excuse to do a little digging and find out what, if anything, the quilters knew about Alan Miller. It wasn't that I didn't trust the detective in charge—it was just that I'd never been good at delegating really important tasks, the ones that needed to be done perfectly. "I'll even pick up the tab. My way of thanking all the volunteers for coming today."

"You make my job so much easier," Fred said. "I wish you were at all my crime scenes."

I glanced at the door, where Richie Faria was frowning at us disapprovingly. "I'm afraid your colleagues aren't so happy that I'm here."

* * *

While Fred continued to mope over the sad remnants of the refreshment table, and Faria engaged in a conversation with Matt over by the entrance to the boardroom, I headed over to where I'd left my messenger bag beneath the appraisal desk, so I could get something to write the lunch orders on.

Most of the quilters were huddled around Dee and Emma. As I approached with my paper and pencil, Emma gave me a guilty look and Dee made a shooing motion at her troops. "Go on now. You all know what to do."

I could have asked everyone to stay, since it would have been easier and faster to get everyone's orders before they broke up, but I thought I'd get more information from them if I could speak to them individually. I remained silent while the quilters wandered off, forming small groups at various workstations.

"We're ordering takeout from the Teriyaki House," I told Dee and Emma. "What would you two like?"

"Just tell them we want our usual," Dee said. "Whoever answers the phone will know what it is."

That was something I still hadn't gotten used to about living in a small town. I wasn't anywhere near as well known as Dee, who'd lived here in Danger Cove her entire life, but many of the local business owners recognized me whenever I stopped in and were able to steer me toward exactly what I wanted before I even knew what I was looking for.

I made a note for Dee's and Emma's order and then asked, "So, what mischief were you setting the quilters off to do?"

"Mischief?" Dee's eyebrows rose. "Me?"

"Yes, you," I said. "I'll tell you the same thing that Detective Ohlsen told me: let the police do their jobs."

Dee laughed. "Yeah, like you're not already meddling yourself."

"I'm not meddling," I insisted. "Just making sure the right questions are being asked and no one's jumping to any conclusions."

"That's all we're doing too," Emma said earnestly. "I promise."

I glanced at the other quilters scattered throughout the room, and they didn't seem to be doing anything suspicious. "What questions do you think need to be asked?"

"We think that poor young man was killed because of the Tree of Life quilt he brought in," Dee said, meaning that it was what she thought, and Emma, always supportive unless her friend's safety was at issue, was going along with the idea. "The police won't think that's a valid motive. Can you convince them to look into it?"

"You'll have to convince me first. Why would someone kill him because of a quilt that belonged to his grandmother and didn't have any real financial value?"

Dee sighed. "I was hoping you'd have an idea. I just know the murder must have had something to do with the quilt. Alan's been in trouble before, but never anything big. So how come, when he's doing something entirely law abiding and ordinary, he gets himself killed?"

In Dee's mind, *everything* was related to quilts. Still, she could be right about Alan's death, and it was definitely a line of inquiry Detective Ohlsen, even with the best of intentions, would never consider. He'd certainly been skeptical about the possibility that Randall Tremain had been killed over a quilt that had a substantial price tag. Alan's grandmother's quilt didn't have that kind of value and would therefore be discounted as a possible motive.

"I'll mention your theory to the detective," I said, "but only if you promise not to do anything about the investigation without checking with me first."

Dee said, "But—"

Emma interrupted, placing a hand on her friend's shoulder for emphasis. "We promise."

I left them to return to their work—not even a murder investigation could come between them and their quilting—and checked in with each of the other workstations to collect lunch orders. A few of the quilters were actually working—cutting, stitching, or ironing the little ornaments—but most were just trading small talk and looking a little dazed by what had happened on the museum's grounds.

Carl Quincy had resumed his stitching at the table closest to the entrance, with his dog at his feet. He stopped working just long enough to place his order and let me know that his dog wouldn't be ready for a meal until later, by which time we both hoped the police would have released everyone to go home.

Trudy was acting as Carl's gopher, taking his finished pieces over to an ironing board and then to wherever they needed to go afterward. She took a moment to consider what she wanted for lunch, but as soon as I'd written it down and asked her if she'd known Alan, she tensed and looked anxiously at the growing chain of pieces that Carl was producing. She produced a seam ripper from the back pocket of her pants and used it to disconnect the chain from the fabric under the presser foot. "I've got to get these over to the ironing station." She glanced around, as if afraid that Jayne Connors was lurking nearby, preparing to pounce on anyone who wasn't keeping up with her assignments.

Trudy had been through enough today, so I didn't insist on an answer, even though I knew that Jayne wasn't in the room. While I'd been chatting with Dee and Emma, Jayne and Meg McLaughlin had stepped out into the hallway together for a private conversation under Richie Faria's close observation. Trudy reached the safety of the nearest ironing station before Jayne and Meg came back inside the boardroom. Jayne's face was red and blotchy, like she'd been crying or at least was furiously embarrassed. Meg wasn't wearing her Santa hat and the red pinafore-style apron any longer, presumably because they were too frivolous for the current somber mood in the room.

I nodded a greeting to Jayne and introduced myself to Meg.

"I've heard so much about you," the quilt instructor said. "Dee and Emma just adore you. They think you're going to be more famous than I am among quilters someday."

"They do have a tendency to get carried away with their enthusiasm," I said. "I doubt an appraiser will ever be more interesting than an artist. They've been very complimentary about you too. I hope I'll get a chance to see some of your work at a show sometime."

"I'd be glad to give you a private showing at my home studio sometime." Meg turned to her assistant. "Maybe Jayne would join us and bring some of her quilts to my house. Then you could see some really extraordinary quilts."

Jayne's face turned redder, but this time it was for happier reasons. When she spoke, she sounded subdued, but nothing seemed to extinguish the shrill tones of her voice. "I wouldn't have finished even one quilt if it weren't for Meg's advice and encouragement."

Out of the corner of my eye, I could see Fred becoming restless. He was going to start licking the sugar off the plates soon if he didn't find some better way to keep his nerves under control. I needed to wrap up my conversation with the last of the quilters and get back to him. I explained to Meg and Jayne about the lunch order I was compiling, donated by someone who preferred to remain anonymous.

Jayne perked up. "They do the most amazing pot stickers. I'll take whatever their lunch special is today, plus a side order of pot stickers."

"I'm not really hungry," Meg said. "I ate a few too many of the Christmas cookies. Perhaps just a salad for me."

"And a side order of pot stickers," Jayne said. "You don't know what you'd be missing if you didn't get them. You moved to Seattle before the Teriyaki House opened. I'll eat them if you decide you don't want them."

Meg nodded her assent. "Please thank the donor for lunch. I just wish it wasn't in such tragic circumstances, so we could enjoy it more."

"I'm sure the donor agrees." I glanced at Fred again, and while he was growing impatient, I thought I had at least another a minute or two before he decided he needed to make an emergency run to the Cinnamon Sugar Bakery. It was a miracle he wasn't diabetic like Carl Quincy.

After talking to all of the other quilters, I had nothing useful for the murder investigation. No one had known Alan Miller well or even particularly noticed his arrival or departure. One of the quilters vaguely recalled selling him the ticket for the appraisal, but only because he was young and male, the only person of that description she'd seen since arriving at the museum this morning. Everyone else had been too busy with their assigned ornament-making tasks to pay attention to anyone else's comings and goings. Meg and Jayne were my last hope for information.

"I don't suppose either of you knew the victim personally."

Meg shook her head. "I used to know everyone in Danger Cove, or at least all of the adults. Alan was too young for me to have known him. He'd have still been a kid when I moved to Seattle."

"I heard he was a drug dealer," Jayne said, her shrill tone sharpening even further with her disdain. "I would never have anything to do with someone like that."

"Even so, you might have noticed what he was up to this morning, since he was memorable as the only young male in the room." Meg and Jayne had been outside the boardroom at various times after Alan left to wait for his ride. I thought one of them might have noticed if Alan had been waiting at the bottom of the stairs, staying in the relative warmth of the hallway, and the person coming to give Alan a ride had come inside to meet him. I didn't want to put any ideas into their heads with a leading question though, so I just asked, "When you were out in the hall, or maybe during a trip to the bathroom, did you see anything unusual relating to Alan?"

The two women looked at each other for a moment, as if each expected the other to speak. Then they turned toward me, shaking their heads.

Meg answered for them. "We were too involved in our own conversation to pay attention to anything else, and when I need to go to the bathroom, there's no time for coherent thought. I don't even recall seeing him leave. I think the only time I noticed him at all was when he was at your appraisal desk, and I wondered what such a young man was doing here with a quilt. Not that men can't be excellent quilters, of course, like Carl Quincy. And Stefan Anderson knows more about quilt history than anyone else here does, except perhaps for you. It's just that it's not very common to see men in their early twenties interested in what used to be called the domestic arts."

I might have continued with my cross-examination, except I caught a glimpse of Fred running a finger through the dusting of sugar on a cookie plate. "I'd better go have this order called in so we don't all collapse from hunger before the food arrives. We wouldn't want to waste all those excellent pot stickers."

* * *

I added an assortment of lunch orders to my list, for Sunny and Stefan, who were still in Gil's office, and Matt, whom I didn't want to interrupt while he was talking to Richie Faria. I handed the paper, along with my credit card, to Fred, who went out into the hall to call in the order. He could still make sure no one left from out there, and he had Richie Faria as backup inside the boardroom, keeping an eye on all of us witnesses.

I was a little surprised that Faria actually let Meg McLaughlin leave for yet another trip to the ladies' room. I would have expected him to insist, on principle, that she needed an escort for the brief walk down the hall. Apparently even he could see there really wasn't anywhere for her to go, not with Fred out in the hall, a clear view of the door to the restrooms, and no way for anyone to escape from the windowless, second-floor space.

Faria cut off his conversation with Matt so he could stand at the entrance with the stoic, silent demeanor of a Buckingham Palace guard. I expected Matt to act like a tourist trying to get one of the Queen's Guard to laugh or otherwise react, but for once he didn't try to get a rise out of anyone. He accepted his dismissal and wandered over to the empty seat next to Carl Quincy at the first sewing machine table.

There wasn't much I could do until the food arrived, so I went over to see if Matt had learned anything from Faria. Matt was a reporter, after all, even if he insisted he was only interested in stories about the arts. Surely he was as curious as I was about what could possibly have led to Alan Miller's untimely death.

By the time I reached the front table, Matt was already surrounded by quilters, most of them a good fifteen to twenty years older than he was. A few of them took selfies with him while he bantered and kept everyone's mind off the uniformed officer at the door and the reason for his presence.

Matt definitely had a way with women. At the quilt show three months ago, I'd seen him graciously rebuff the matchmaking efforts of the quilters who'd wanted to introduce him to their daughters or granddaughters, and he'd pretended not to notice the other quilters who were infatuated with him.

I wasn't entirely sure what they all saw in him. It wasn't just that he was a novelty, as a male vastly outnumbered by women in the room. Carl Quincy hadn't attracted any groupies. Matt was more gregarious than Carl, although given the number of pictures being taken, the attraction seemed to be primarily based on Matt's appearance, not on his conversational skills.

I hadn't imagined it earlier today; Matt's looks really had improved during his absence. His hair was different than the last time I saw him. It had been cut and styled within the last two or three weeks, instead of being several months overdue for a trim. Of course, some things didn't change. Matt still favored the same brand of excessively-pocketed cargo pants and odd-colored sport shirts.

Matt politely encouraged the last selfie-taker to move along, and then he turned to me. I'd never really believed that anyone could express hunger for another person just through his eyes and facial expression, but he was definitely looking at me as if we were lovers reunited after a long separation. Of course, he probably used the same expression on all of his groupies. He'd probably learned to fake it while posing for the camera.

I'd never been a groupie, and I had no intention of starting now. I returned his gaze coolly.

It didn't seem to bother him. In fact, his smile widened even more. "Life is always an adventure when we're together."

I couldn't help the way my spirits lifted. He really was charming, and I was as susceptible to his blarney as all the other women in the room. And then I remembered the three months when he hadn't called.

"People die when we're together."

"I guess I've got my work cut out for me if you associate me with death." Matt gestured for me to sit next to him. "I like a challenge though."

I dropped into the empty chair while I considered how to respond to his flirting. I wasn't in the market for anything more than a friendship with him or anyone else these days anyway. Friends were good. Everyone needed them, and they'd been shown to reduce stress. Romantic relationships, on the other hand, generally caused a huge spike in stress levels, at least in their early stages. Oh, sure, they had their health benefits too, with all those endorphins and serotonin being released, but I needed to get my medical condition under better control before I even considered dating again. Otherwise, I'd be passing out left and right, which, in addition to scaring off potential lovers, also tended to cause bruises, concussions, and broken bones. No man, least of all an unreliable one, was worth that kind of pain.

I deliberately pretended to misunderstand Matt's last comment. "Would it be a big enough challenge if I asked you to help me make sure the police are on the right track today? I saw you talking to Richie Faria. Did he tell you anything about what's going on downstairs?"

Matt hesitated for the briefest moment before accepting the change of subject. "He wouldn't say anything. Apparently it's against the rules for responding officers to say anything substantive to reporters. All he can do is refer me to the lead detective."

"Seriously? And you let him get away with that?"

"Of course not. I didn't need him to say anything. His body language told me everything he knew. All I had to do was ask leading questions and watch his response. As best I can tell, their theory is that it's a case of a known troublemaker hanging around with the wrong people and reaping the consequences."

"That seems awfully simplistic. A one-size-fits-all theory of crime," I said. "Of course, Dee and Emma think Alan was killed because of the quilt, and that's just another flavor of one-size-fits-all solutions. Everything is about quilts for them."

"It's as good a theory as the official one," he said. "But you're right. I think it's more complicated than either one. What's your theory? I saw you talking to everyone, and it looked like you were asking more than, 'What do you want for lunch?'"

I glanced at Richie Faria, standing at attention beside the door. "Was I that obvious?"

"No," Matt said. "Faria wasn't paying you any attention. He thinks you're nothing but a clueless meddler, not worth watching. Just shows you what a fool he is. And I wasn't about to tell him what you were up to. You owe me for not blowing your cover, so tell me what you found out."

"Nothing, I'm afraid. No one saw anything, no one actually knew Alan except by reputation, and they're all in a bit of shock."

"I think someone in this room is in more shock than everyone else."

My voice rose in surprise. "You think one of the quilters did it?"

Carl Quincy stiffened at the far end of the table.

"It's just a theory," Matt said. "But think about where Alan was killed. I think he knew his killer and wasn't afraid to be alone with him—or her—in a secluded area where he'd essentially be trapped within a confined space."

"It wouldn't be the first time that someone underestimated a quilter."

"Exactly. He must have thought the killer was harmless. From what I've heard, Alan was a streetwise kid, so he'd have stayed out in the open if he thought the other person might want to attack him. It's not easy to stab a person if the victim has some warning and an open path to run away."

"What would you know about a stabbing?" I hadn't looked at the corpse closely enough to see any details other than Alan's unseeing eyes and a vague impression of blood. "You keep telling me you're nothing but a lowly arts reporter."

"People always assume reporters are interested in crimes, so I hear all sorts of stuff. But I really do prefer reporting on art." Matt looked down at the bed of the sewing machine for a moment. "Forget about my history. Let's just say I've seen a lot of things, most of them completely unrelated to being a reporter. Trust me when I say I know what a stabbing victim looks like."

"Okay, but why would a quilter stab Alan Miller?"

"That's your job to figure out," Matt said. "I was hoping you could fill in the motivation from what you'd learned."

"Sorry. All I got was lunch orders and a whole lot of 'I know nothing.'"

"Not your fault," Matt said. "No one does her best work on an empty stomach. We can both try again after we've eaten. Until then, I'm going to make some ornaments. What about you?"

"Nothing that involves a sewing machine. They can be as deadly as a knife."

"Never thought you'd be such a chicken." Matt grabbed a red square and a white square, but instead of stitching a seam close to one edge of the paired-up pieces as I'd seen Carl do, he stitched a diagonal line across the squares. "It's easy. See?"

I pointed at the white board. "Your work doesn't look anything like the diagrams or like any of the other pieces I've seen around the room."

"I prefer to make my own designs." He took another pair of squares and made another random, but admittedly straight, diagonal stitching line, and then repeated the process with two more pairs of squares. "Be right back."

He dashed off to an ironing board, did some quick pressing, then jogged over to a cutting table, did something I couldn't see, and then came back with his stitched pieces trimmed down to squares. They still didn't look anything like the diagram on the white board. Instead of being precisely split down the middle into two identical but different-colored triangles, his squares were divided along a diagonal line into two unequal sections, sometimes with more red and sometimes with more white.

Matt laid his pieced squares on the table, alternating them with some plain squares of fabric. He placed a red square in the middle and white ones in the four corners. I could see a vague resemblance to the diagram on the wall, but instead of forming a star with four identical triangular points, his star had four points that were all a slightly different size and shape from each other.

A few quilters wandered over, and one of them said something about Gwen Marston and *Liberated Quiltmaking*. I'd heard of the iconic book, but I hadn't personally viewed any quilts made in that spontaneous and intentionally imperfect style.

When Matt finished his little star, he handed it to me. It really did look quite nice, pulsing with more energy than the precisely pieced blocks. I doubted Meg and Jayne would approve, although when I turned it over, the seams did appear to be perfectly even at a scant quarter inch.

When I put the block down on the table, Matt searched his pockets until he found a pen with indelible ink. He signed a white corner square with *Matteo*, and handed it to one of the women who'd been admiring his handiwork. Admiring something about him anyway.

He asked her, "Would you get this ironed, and pass it along to whoever's layering the blocks for finishing?"

The woman took the block and carried it over to a nearby ironing board as carefully as if it were made of spun glass.

CHAPTER SEVEN

———

Matt didn't need my help with his quiltmaking or his groupies, so I stood to go see if I could help Gil, who had returned from her office and was growing increasingly frustrated with Richie Faria. He was apparently enforcing his *can't talk to mere civilians while I'm guarding the room* rule even when it came to dealing with the one person who could best help him keep the situation under control.

Before I could go join Gil, Emma called my name and waved me over to where she and Dee were working. Emma kept her voice low and confidential, making her hard to hear over the sewing machine motors. "It's great to see you and Matt working together again. He couldn't stop talking about you after the quilt show, right up to the minute he left town, and then he asked about you as soon as he got back yesterday."

So Matt hadn't just been gone a few days, he'd been gone the entire time I'd been wondering when he was going to call. "That's a long time to be away. I can't imagine the *Cove Chronicles* sending him off on assignment for three months. Where was he?"

Beside Emma, Dee suddenly felt the need to study the pieces of fabric she was about to stitch together, and Emma's eyes developed a frozen, deer-in-the-headlights look.

Finally, Emma said, "I forgot. We're not supposed to talk about it. He made us promise. I think he finds it embarrassing."

"Ridiculous man," Dee said, patting my hand apologetically. "But we did promise. You'll have to ask him yourself."

"I will." No matter what Dee and Emma seemed to think, I was convinced Matt's flirting was nothing more than a part of his job. Once he realized he didn't need to play the game and just told me what he wanted, we might actually be able to be friends. "In the meantime though, there really isn't anything for us to work on together. Not while we're cooped up here, with no idea of whether the police have already caught the culprit."

"They couldn't possibly have the killer in custody," Dee said. "It's got to be one of the quilters, and we're all accounted for. I don't like thinking of my guild as harboring a killer, but who else could it be?"

"Poor Sunny," Emma said. "She's going to be the prime suspect, isn't she?"

"I'm afraid so, just because she found the body."

"That's not the only reason for them to suspect her." Dee handed Emma some pieces to carry over to a nearby ironing board. "Sunny knew Alan and wasn't on the best of terms with him."

I couldn't imagine what could have brought the two of them—a physical therapist/entrepreneur and an unemployed millennial—together and then set them at odds. "How do they even know each other?"

"Sunny interviewed Alan for a job at the hospital's physical therapy department," Dee said, "and she declined to hire him. She even left the job unfilled rather than offer it to him. He wasn't happy about it."

"That sounds like an incentive for him to attack her, not the other way around."

"Maybe he did, and Sunny killed him in self-defense," Dee said. "She's really strong. Even more than you might think from looking at her. She's got to be for her job. I know, because she worked with me three years ago when I injured my hip, and I saw her working with patients the size of professional football players."

"Let's just keep this theory between us for now. You remember the drill from before: answer the detective's questions, but don't volunteer any information they don't specifically ask for, and if you get nervous, just stop talking except to say you want to call your attorney."

Emma returned in time to hear my warning. "I remember," she said with a shudder.

Dee nodded. "We'll just tell them we want to talk to you."

"I'm not your lawyer," I said, exasperated. "If you need to talk to an attorney, it should be someone who has experience with criminal law and isn't herself a potential suspect."

"There's nothing for us to worry about," Dee said. "I'm confident you and Matt will figure it all out. I just hope you can do it quickly. If Meg can't get leave on schedule this afternoon, she'll remember the delay next year when we invite her back for another guild event, and she might not be willing to come. Even the prospect of a free night at the Ocean View B&B won't be enough to tempt her. The place is charming, on a cliff overlooking the ocean, and the innkeeper, Bree Milford, is a lovely woman. We want that experience to be what Meg remembers about Danger Cove, not a police interrogation that kept her here for hours and hours."

It wasn't worth explaining, yet again, that there really wasn't much that Matt or I could do. Dee and Emma thought we were invincible, much as they viewed themselves when it came to quilting. "I can't speak for Matt, but I'll do what I can to keep the investigation moving forward."

* * *

Judging by the way Gil was now humming along with the background Christmas music, through gritted teeth, she'd gotten nowhere with the stone-faced Richie Faria while I was talking to Dee and Emma. Gil had abandoned Faria and was mingling with the volunteers. Matt was also doing his best to entertain the quilters, holding an impromptu discussion of his quilting techniques at the white board.

At the other end of the room, trouble was brewing over the ironing board where Stefan had been assigned earlier. Jayne was shrilly lecturing another quilter, this one about my age, with a businesslike short haircut and a strong, square face. Jayne's latest victim had far more backbone than Trudy and, judging by her narrowed eyes and pinched-shut lips, was holding on to her temper by a thread much flimsier than the top-quality cotton that ran through the sewing machines.

Gil hadn't noticed the incipient explosion, so I hurried over to intervene. "I don't think we've met," I said to the irritated woman holding a steaming iron in her hands as if she were going to bash Jayne over the head with it. I didn't want to think about what Richie Faria would do if there was a murder or even just an assault right in front of him. "I'm Keely Fairchild. The appraiser. I'm no good at sewing or even ironing, but you look like you could use some help. Is there something I can do?"

"I don't need any help," the woman said in a clipped tone, addressing Jayne instead of me. "I know what I'm doing."

"Good. Then I can borrow Jayne to help me." I hooked my arm around Jayne's elbow and tugged her in the direction of the cutting table. "I've always wanted to know how to use a rotary cutter. Maybe I'd be better at that than sewing or ironing."

Jayne looked at me skeptically. "It's not something you should do without some training. The blades are extremely sharp."

"That's why I need you to show me how to do it."

"Well, I guess that would be okay." Jayne started off on what sounded like a rehearsed spiel about how to hold the cutter and making sure to always cut away from the body, never toward it.

Once we reached the cutting table, I only half listened, since I didn't actually trust myself with the cutter for the exact reason Jayne had mentioned: it was sharp and dangerous, and that wasn't a good combination in the hands of someone who might pass out unexpectedly.

My mind drifted, and I saw Meg return from her latest trip to the bathroom to join Gil in reassuring the quilters that the police had everything under the control. Richie Faria got a call on his police-issued radio. While he answered it, he beckoned for Carl Quincy to come over to the door. Carl gave his service dog an order to heel, and the two of them went over to consult with Faria. Judging by their actions, the gist of the conversation was that Carl should keep an eye on the quilters while Faria stepped out into the hall to continue his radio conversation. Did Faria really think we were going to erupt into a riot without the constant supervision of a professional trained in crowd control?

"Hey." Jayne's shrill voice interrupted my thoughts. "If you're not going to pay attention, it's not worth my time trying to teach you."

"I'm sorry." I hadn't meant to be rude. I just couldn't concentrate with everything else running through my mind. "Perhaps it would be better if I waited until a less stressful time to learn how to use a rotary cutter. I couldn't help noticing that something seems to be happening with the police. Faria deputized Carl to keep an eye on the room."

"And who's going to watch Carl?" Jayne said, carefully setting down the rotary cutter she'd been using for her demonstration.

"I doubt Faria thinks a retired officer needs watching."

Jayne's already disapproving face took on an even more sour appearance. "If that's the sort of shoddy police work that's happening here, they'll never find that poor young man's killer."

"Faria's just a rookie," I said. "The real work is being supervised by Detective Bud Ohlsen, and he's a good guy."

"A job is only as good as its weakest link," Jayne said. "Someone needs to tell Faria that Carl is as much a suspect as anyone else in the room. Probably has more motive than anyone else, actually."

"I know he didn't trust Alan, but there's no indication Carl was ever a rogue cop who went around Danger Cove killing everyone who annoyed him. Why would he do it when he's retired?"

"He has a lot more motive than simple mistrust," Jayne said. "I didn't think to mention it before when you asked about when Alan left to catch his ride. Something happened before that, the first time Alan left the room. He kicked Carl's dog on the way past, or at least that's what Carl claimed when he caught up to Alan in the hallway. Meg and I were near the door, and we heard Carl say he'd kill Alan if he so much as looked at the dog again."

I didn't have any pets myself, but I knew how attached people could be to them. Add in the extra level of bonding with a service dog, and I couldn't simply brush off Carl's statement as an exaggeration or a thoughtless phrase. It bothered me that he hadn't mentioned the incident with the dog when he'd confessed that he'd been near the crime scene right around the time of the murder. As long as he'd volunteered he'd had the opportunity, why hadn't he mentioned he also had a motive, unless he'd done more than just threaten Alan?

Still, it was all just speculation, and the last thing we needed today was Jayne accusing an ex-cop of murder.

"I'm sure the police will consider all the evidence, including the altercation between Carl and Alan, and they'll be able to decide whether it's relevant."

"I hope so," Jayne said. "I just think things should be done right, that's all."

I agreed with her in principle, even if I knew better than to say it out loud. I was doing my best to overcome the need to make sure everything proceeded smoothly and efficiently, even when it wasn't my responsibility. I had to let go of that stress if I didn't want to keep passing out.

"Detective Ohlsen really is good at his job," I said.

"I hope so," Jayne said. "I mean, I know *I* didn't have anything to do with the murder, so whoever's arrested, it won't have anything to do with me. But I'd hate to see some innocent person traumatized by being suspected of murder. Today has been enough of a mess, and I just want to finish up here and go home."

"Once the police start taking statements, they should be able to release everyone who has a confirmed alibi pretty quickly," I said. "Can someone vouch for where you were the whole time Alan was outside?"

"I was right here, helping people." Jayne rattled off a detailed list of at least a dozen people, the exact times she'd been with them, and what they'd been doing that was so desperately wrong that she'd needed to intervene. "I'm sure they'll remember."

I was sure they would too, although not in the positive sense that Jayne meant. Still, there was one good thing about her abrasive personality: no one would ever forget where Jayne had been when it came time to providing an alibi. Of course, her witnesses might not be too enthusiastic about vouching for her, and if they were sufficiently annoyed, they might well be tempted to deny knowing where Jayne had been, especially if they could legitimately say that they had a less clear memory of the exact time of the interaction than Jayne had.

All in all, I suspected Jayne might not have as easy a time as she expected with proving she couldn't possibly have killed Alan. I didn't know what Bud Ohlsen would think, but I certainly considered her a suspect.

* * *

Faria returned from the hallway, his chest puffed up with self-importance. He had a quick word with Carl Quincy, who nodded and abandoned his sewing machine to head over to where Gil was chatting with a group of quilters at the refreshments table.

Faria whistled sharply. "Listen up, everyone. I've been assigned to collect everyone's contact information. I'll be taking over the desk in the back of the room, and Carl Quincy will be in charge of escorting everyone over to see me. I expect all of you ladies to do as he asks, just as if I were the one asking you."

If Faria was going to be using the desk where I'd done the appraisals, I needed to get my messenger bag out of his way and make sure I'd packed up all my supplies. I hurried over there before he could make up some new rule of police procedure that might prevent me from collecting my own personal property. Fortunately, the only things I'd left out were the completed applications for quilts to be added to the museum's registry. I was stuffing the papers into my bag to give to Gil later, when Faria dropped into the chair I'd used earlier.

"We might as well start with your information." Faria's tone turned decidedly sarcastic. "Unless you've solved it already, of course. In that case, you could save us all a lot of time and effort."

"I don't have any idea who killed Alan Miller, but I would like to have a chat with Detective Ohlsen. If the murder has anything to do with either the museum or the people here for the workshop, he might have some questions about the quilting community that I could answer for him."

"That won't be necessary." Faria pulled out a little notepad and gestured toward the two chairs across from him. "Have a seat."

I hadn't realized until now just how awkwardly the chairs were placed. Anyone sitting in them would be staring into the corner of the room, like a child in time-out, unable to see the activity behind her. It wasn't just security professionals who liked to sit with their backs to a wall in order to keep an eye out for trouble. I'd always done the same thing as a trial attorney, making sure I had the best possible view of the people who mattered: the judge and jury.

I didn't like this seating arrangement, but there really wasn't any other option. Faria would undoubtedly consider resistance to any of his orders to be tantamount to a confession of murder. Besides, it shouldn't take long to give him my contact information.

"All right." Faria's pen was poised over his notebook. "Your full name and contact information. And spell out anything that might not be obvious."

"It's the same as before." I spoke slowly, giving him time to write it all down, providing my name, address, phone numbers, and email address.

He repeated the information back to me, and I grudgingly gave him credit for recording it accurately. He might not like me, but that didn't stop him from doing his job.

He looked up from his notebook. "Did you know the victim? Or anything about his past brushes with the law?"

That question went beyond his assigned role of collecting contact information. In someone else, I might have thought it was just personal curiosity, but his formal tone suggested he thought he was qualified to get additional information from the witnesses and would be writing down my answers. I doubted Detective Ohlsen had actually given him that much authority. He would have cringed to hear the way Faria was telling a witness information that I might not already have, namely that the victim had a criminal past. Now I really wanted a word with Ohlsen, before Faria could unwittingly alter all of the witnesses' memories of the morning's events.

Fortunately, I'd already heard about Alan's shady past, so Faria hadn't done anything more than confirm by implication that the initial theory of the case was that the young man's past had caught up with him. It wouldn't hurt to tell Faria what little I knew about Alan, and clamming up would only cause more problems. Perhaps if I cooperated, Faria would let more information slip.

"I only met Alan Miller briefly. He was here to have a quilt appraised. I did the appraisal, and he went outside to call for a ride home, came back in for some refreshments, and then left again. It was maybe thirty or forty minutes later when I heard Sunny calling for help, right after she found the body."

"You don't know that's when she found the body," he said, smirking as if he'd caught me in some huge lie. He was acting like a brand-new lawyer doing his first, real-life cross-examination without understanding which inconsistencies mattered and which were best ignored or saved for a more effective time to point them out. "She could have found the body earlier than that."

"And held off hysterical screams for more than a few seconds?" My eyebrows rose. "That seems fairly unlikely."

"I'm just saying." Faria underlined something in his notes. "You're editorializing."

"I know the difference between a statement of fact and an opinion." I'd prepared enough witnesses on that issue. "So. Just the facts. It was no more than forty minutes between seeing him leave here and hearing the screams. I ran outside with Matt Viera. I saw Sunny and then saw the body on the ground. There was a great deal of blood, and Alan wasn't moving."

"That's better," Faria said. "Where were you between the time the victim left and the time you heard the screams?"

"Right here, doing appraisals and then mingling with the other volunteers." I pointed over my shoulder and a bit to the right. "If you want an alibi, check with Dee Madison, Emma Quinn, and Matt Viera."

"Emma Quinn? Isn't she the old biddy with a rap sheet? Suspected of murdering Randall Tremain?"

"She has a criminal record for shoplifting." I swallowed my irritation and kept my voice even. "You'll recall, however, that she did not have anything to do with Randall Tremain's murder, and she was gracious enough not to sue the town for false arrest."

"We had reasonable cause," he said defensively.

"Perhaps," I said. "And now that you've got my name and contact information, I think we're done."

Faria clearly wanted to ask me more questions, but he had to know he'd gone quite a few steps beyond his actual authority. He hesitated, probably weighing how much of a fuss I was likely to make if he pushed me any further and whether I might get him pulled off this assignment completely.

"If that's how you want to play it," he said, "it's fine with me. For now, just stay in this room and don't talk about the incident with any of the other witnesses. Wouldn't want anyone's memory being altered."

Too late for that, I thought. Except he'd been the one giving me information instead of the other way around. Not that I'd learned anything truly useful talking to the various quilters. No one seemed to know anything about the murder. After all, the assault had happened outside, and there were no windows overlooking the parking lot. It was entirely possible that the only person who had seen anything useful for figuring out who had killed Alan was the killer herself, and she certainly wasn't going to admit to that knowledge.

I stood up and saw that Carl had escorted ten of the quilters over to the chairs along the wall, where people had waited much more happily for their appraisals earlier. Carl stood at the front of the line, leaning against the wall. His dog came over and nudged him. Carl unhooked his water bottle, went to take a drink, only to shake it, apparently surprised to find it was empty. He patted the dog's head and murmured what I thought was "in a minute," and then resumed chatting quietly with Trudy, who was seated in the first chair.

Despite Carl's attempts to keep Trudy calm, she looked terrified, and her face had turned red again, this time with anxiety, I thought, rather than embarrassment. If I weren't a witness of sorts myself, and even a potential suspect until someone confirmed my alibi, I'd have been tempted to whisper something reassuring into Trudy's ear. In the circumstances though, all I could do was smile encouragingly.

I needed to talk to Ohlsen before Trudy fell under Faria's influence. Carl already knew about Alan's history, so he'd be safe enough as the next person to be interviewed. That would give me time to find Fred and get a leash placed on Faria. "Are you going to interview Carl next?"

Faria laughed, clearly amused by the foolishness of an amateur like me. "I know how to get in touch with Carl, and it's obvious he's got nothing to tell me about what happened, or he would have done it already."

If it had been Detective Ohlsen who was that dismissive of interviewing Carl, I'd have mentioned what I knew about the verbal altercation I'd witnessed and the threat that Jayne had told me about. Faria, however, didn't need to know that information, and it wasn't my responsibility to teach him how to be a detective. Instead, I needed to find a way to have a chat with Ohlsen before Faria did too much damage to the investigation. Fred would be able to arrange it.

"If you're done with me, I'd like to go see what's happening with our lunch delivery."

"Sure, sure." Faria gestured for Trudy to take my seat.

Carl dropped into Trudy's vacated chair. As I approached him, I noticed that his dog was whining, and he had the stuffed blue nylon tube in his mouth, instead of hanging loose from his collar.

"Oh, great," Carl said just before he slid out of his chair, hitting his head on the wood floor with a solid thump.

CHAPTER EIGHT

———

I hadn't realized that Sunny and Stefan had returned to the boardroom while I'd had my back to the doors, but Sunny was kneeling beside the unconscious Carl before I recovered enough from my surprise to be able to move. She sent Stefan off to see if anyone had a hard candy in her purse and snapped at Faria to call 9-1-1 for an ambulance, with instructions to tell the dispatcher that the victim appeared to be having some kind of diabetic event.

She had the situation under control, so I stayed out of the way, returning to the desk to stand beside Trudy. I'd been on the receiving end of well-intentioned but clueless attention after a few of my syncope events, so I knew better than to try to help.

One good thing came out of Carl's passing out: Richie Faria was too busy dealing with the crisis to interrogate Trudy. On the other hand, Trudy was so pale, I thought she might be the next one to pass out.

"Is he going to be okay?" Trudy asked me. "He was so kind to me."

"Help is on the way, and until then, Sunny is a nurse, so she knows what to do." Even as I spoke, the paramedics came trotting through the door. I went around the desk to where Faria had left his notepad, and sat across from Trudy. The dog had dropped the blue nylon tube and was hunkered down next to his master's head, but I thought he seemed less frantic than before. "Drag your chair over here with me, and you can keep an eye on things without being in the way."

Trudy plopped down next to me, and we watched as Carl regained consciousness and the paramedics wrapped a blood pressure cuff on his arm and asked him a bunch of questions. His responses were groggy but coherent. I recognized from my own experiences the moment when he became fully aware that he was the center of all sorts of unwanted attention. He struggled to sit up, while the paramedics insisted that he remain lying still until they'd finished their tests. I recognized that little *pas de deux* too. The lawyer in me understood that the paramedics needed to be sure there wouldn't be a relapse, but the patient in me cringed at the self-conscious helplessness Carl had to feel. It had to be even worse for him than for me, because of his masculine ego and a lifetime of relying on his physical strength. I wasn't a weakling, but my self-image had always been more connected to the strength of my brain than to the strength of my body.

Carl insisted he was fine and claimed that Rusty's having dropped the bringsel—so that was what that blue nylon tube hanging from the dog's collar was called—indicated that there was nothing seriously wrong with him now. He'd just become dehydrated, or possibly his blood sugar had dropped too far, and the candy that Sunny had given him had taken care of the problem.

"Better safe than sorry," the overly perky blonde paramedic, who looked to be about twelve years old, said. That sort of cheerful but implacable insistence might have worked on some patients, but I had a feeling that Carl saw her as I would have: an annoying housefly buzzing around his head. Only his lifelong commitment to law and order was keeping him from swatting her away.

Trudy stood. "It's all right, Carl. You should go get checked out. I'll be fine without you here. I'll be strong for you."

Trudy still looked pale, and I thought worrying about Carl was upsetting her more than the possibility of being interrogated by the police. Apparently Carl thought so too, because he nodded begrudgingly. "All right. But only if Rusty here can ride in the ambulance with me."

* * *

I still needed to talk to Detective Ohlsen, but I couldn't leave to find him until I was confident Faria wouldn't traumatize Trudy. The last thing we needed right now was another person passing out.

I decided to stick around and keep an eye on Trudy until Faria was done with her. I gave up my seat behind the desk to take Carl's spot leaning against the wall at the front of the line, where I could listen to the interrogation. Trudy took her chair back to the other side just in time for Faria to return and resume his duties. Carl's incident appeared to have dimmed Faria's enthusiasm for his work though, since he limited his questions to the basic ones he'd been assigned to do, instead of trying to do real detective work. I couldn't be sure whether it was just because he assumed Trudy was an airhead, or if he had truly reformed. I still needed to have a chat with Ohlsen about reining Faria in.

Once Faria let Trudy leave the hot seat, I turned to observe the rest of the room. The mood was even more somber now than it had been immediately after Alan's death. Gil was holding nervous hands, patting shoulders, and occasionally providing the vocals for the music in the background. I wasn't sure when she'd left to take care of it, but at some point, she'd replaced this morning's upbeat music with more somber instrumental music, like the classic orchestral version of "Silent Night," which was playing now.

Gil must have felt me looking at her. She gestured for me to follow her over to the door, where we could talk somewhat privately.

That was where I was headed anyway, since I was hoping I could catch sight of Fred from there. I crossed the room and managed a quick peek out into the deserted hallway before Gil bent down to whisper, "I'm so sorry you got dragged into this. But I'm also glad you're here. I can count on you to help me keep everyone from panicking."

"It's probably too late for that." I glanced at where Trudy was huddled behind the sewing machine Carl had been using earlier. She was patting the top of the sewing machine, as if reassuring it that Carl would return to operate it again.

The anxious edge to Gil's voice reclaimed my full attention. "They're all looking to me for answers, and I don't know what to tell them. My business school instructors didn't teach us anything about police investigations. The legal classes I took were all focused on things like contracts and intellectual property, not murder."

I wished I could offer some reassurance, but I was outside my comfort zone too. "The only thing I know about dealing with detectives is that if you're going to talk to them, it's best to tell the truth, and if you can't do that without incriminating yourself, you should refuse to say anything at all until your lawyer is seated next to you. I imagine everyone knows that much these days, just from watching television."

"I wonder if I should get a lawyer before I talk to the detective," Gil said.

"I'd never tell anyone not to get a lawyer, but I can't see why anyone would think you might have killed Alan."

"I'm not worried about that." Gil pulled me just outside the room into the hallway, where we were less likely to be overheard. "For at least half an hour before Sunny screamed, I was down in the museum's lobby, dealing with a visitor who had some questions the staff couldn't answer. One of the museum's security guards was with me the whole time, and the interior cameras are working, so it will be easy to prove that I wasn't anywhere near the parking lot at the time of the murder."

"Then why are you worried?"

"This is privileged, right?" She peered back into the boardroom until she was apparently reassured that no one was within earshot and then turned to me again. "I'm saying this to you as a lawyer."

"Of course." I was still licensed, even if I didn't have an active practice. And I wanted to know what Gil was so worried about. "Is it about the cameras? Are you thinking about the museum's potential civil liability for not having the cameras working out back?"

"Exactly," Gil said. "The detectives have probably already gone to the control room and found that the exterior cameras aren't working, but I'd rather not discuss it with them until I've gotten legal advice."

"That's understandable. Detective Ohlsen knows better than to keep asking questions after someone's requested legal representation, and I'm pretty sure Faria doesn't have the authority to collect anything except names and addresses, so you can be even more emphatic with him."

"I just hope it will turn out that the murder didn't have anything to do with the museum or the lack of video surveillance. People should feel safe when they come here, and I've been trying to convince the board to take security more seriously."

"I'm not sure what else you can do," I said. "You do have video surveillance usually, there's security staff inside the building, and patrol cops like Fred Fields maintain a solid presence all along Main Street."

"Still, there must be something more we could do. You'd be amazed how much petty crime goes on, even in a little town like this. Not committed by the local residents usually, and not even by most of the visitors, but wherever there are tourists, there are pickpockets and people trying to steal identities. We've had a few visitors report that their wallet was stolen while they were here, but we couldn't find any evidence of it on our cameras. It might have happened before the visitors came in here, and they just didn't realize it until they went to buy something in the museum shop, especially if they'd prepaid their admission tickets online."

That definitely changed the cheerful, positive image I'd had of the holiday-shopping tourists I'd passed on the way to the museum. Now it felt like the dangers that had given rise to the town's name had moved inland. Unwary shoppers could fall victim not to eddies, rocks, and sharks but to pickpockets, thugs, and killers.

Was it possible that criminals were specifically stalking the museum's patrons? The stolen wallets could have been due to criminals lurking outside the building, possibly even in the parking lot. In that case, then maybe the police theory of what had happened today was right. Alan could have bumped into a less-than-savory friend outside, someone other than the person giving him a ride, only to have a falling-out that had ended in murder. That would explain why Alan had been way over in the corner of the parking lot instead of out front on the sidewalk. If he'd been conspiring with a criminal, they wouldn't have wanted to be in plain sight of anyone who might be walking or driving past the museum.

It was just a theory though, and I didn't want to worry Gil any more than necessary. "You can't blame yourself for everything that criminals do. There's no way to prevent crime completely."

"I'm still going to look into increasing our security," Gil said. "Maybe some sort of fail-safe option for situations when the main cameras are out, like now."

I was distracted by footsteps coming up the stairs, and a moment later Fred arrived, shadowed by a young uniformed officer I didn't recognize. Both men were laden down with the black-and-silver take-out bags from the Teriyaki House. The corner of one more bag, this one the distinctive pink and brown of the Cinnamon Sugar Bakery, stuck out from Fred's jacket pocket.

Gil and I scurried back inside the room before Fred could say anything about our being in the hallway. The two men carried the bags over to the conference table, and then the younger officer left without a word. Fred stayed beside the table, wearing the worried expression that I knew was typical of him in the aftermath of a crime he hadn't been able to prevent. I was sure he didn't mean to scare people away from claiming their lunches, but that was the effect he was having.

I told Gil, "Everyone will feel better after they've had something to eat," and I headed over to see if I could get Fred to relax a little.

Gil came with me. "I hope so. Did you know I paid for a good chunk of my education by working in food service? I never thought I'd use those skills again, but at least it will keep me busy while the police do their work."

As soon as we arrived at the table, Fred patted his bulging pocket again and then pulled out my credit card to return it. "I'll be at the door if you need me."

Each of the boxes from the Teriyaki House had a neat label describing its contents, making them easy to identify. I found the ones for myself, Matt, Stefan, and Sunny and then borrowed a pencil from Gil to mark them with our names.

Trudy was the first to join us at the refreshments table. She reached for one of the bags to peer inside, setting her charm bracelet to jangling. "Do you need some help?"

"I never turn away volunteers." Gil placed a stack of the black-and-silver containers in Trudy's startled hands. "You can deliver the lunches. There's a description on each lid. Just call it out and take it to whoever claims it."

The first order turned out to be Jayne's, and I was impressed by the way Trudy straightened her shoulders and trotted over to deliver the food to the woman who'd been so mean to her earlier. Carl would have been proud of her.

I turned to Gil. "Where did you learn to manage people by keeping them busy? In business school or in food service?"

"Neither one," Gil said. "I'm the oldest of six kids, and that automatically made me the designated babysitter. I quickly figured out that as long as my siblings were busy, they didn't have time to get into trouble. It works with employees, volunteers, and board members too."

"I wish it worked on cops," I said. "I need to have a chat with Detective Ohlsen."

CHAPTER NINE

———

I left Gil to take care of the food distribution and went to see if I could get a message to Ohlsen. Fred was more than willing to step out into the hallway to discuss it, since then he could dig his cupcake out of the bakery bag and nibble on it.

"Richie Faria is going way beyond just collecting names and contact information," I told him. "Could you let Detective Ohlsen know about it? Faria really doesn't have the experience to question anyone at a murder scene, and I doubt Ohlsen asked him to do it."

"I'll take care of it." Fred swiped at a bit of frosting on his upper lip. "Is that all you needed?"

I wanted to stay and listen while he talked to Detective Ohlsen, just to make sure my message was passed along accurately, but I also needed to stay on good terms with Fred, so I couldn't question his abilities. I needed an excuse to stay outside the noisy boardroom where I might be able to eavesdrop on the conversation inconspicuously.

"I'd like to use the ladies' room, if it's okay." If I timed it right, I might be able to catch at least part of Fred's conversation with the detective.

"Sure," Fred said, reaching for his cell phone. "I should have an answer from Ohlsen by the time you get back."

I headed down the hallway, aware of Fred watching me. He wasn't as obsessed with following the rules as the rookie Faria was but was thorough in his own low-key way. He would be able to report, if asked, that he had kept an eye on me, even though he had to know I wasn't going to make a sudden turn and race down the stairs.

I passed Meg, who had just left the restroom. I spent the bare minimum of time in the ladies' room and returned in time to hear Fred repeating my concerns about Faria almost verbatim. There was a moment of silence, and then Fred said, "I'll send Faria out to you right away."

He put his phone back into his jacket pocket. "I'll be taking over the interviews. Bud's going to have a chat with Faria."

"Thanks." Fred was no detective, but unlike the rookie, he knew his limits, and he was good with people. I couldn't fix what had happened so far today, but at least with Faria reassigned, we should be able to get back to some semblance of normalcy.

* * *

Fred followed me into the boardroom. I paused in the doorway while he went to the back of the room to replace Faria. Almost everyone had claimed their lunch and was quietly eating. I spotted Stefan and Sunny seated together on the floor in the far back corner, past the conference table and separated by the width of the room from the desk where Faria was resisting his eviction.

I scooped up Sunny's and Stefan's lunches and carried them over to where Sunny was leaning against Stefan with her eyes closed. Stefan seemed tense, as if he were on guard duty.

I wasn't sure if Sunny was awake, so I crouched down next to Stefan and whispered, "How's she doing?"

"She's strong," Stefan said in an equally soft voice. "She'll be okay eventually."

Sunny opened her eyes and straightened away from Stefan. "I'm fine now." She laughed ruefully. "I wanted to be an ER nurse originally, but I could never handle the sight of blood. I passed out dozens of times before I finally accepted that physical therapy was a better career for me."

"I probably would have passed out in an operating room too." I handed Sunny one of the take-out containers.

I gave Stefan the second one, which he placed next to him on the wood floor. His face remained tight with anxiety, and his eyes looked a bit dazed, as if he'd been the one to find the body, not Sunny. She, on the other hand, looked completely recovered. Maybe Stefan's seemingly over-the-top praise of her was actually an accurate representation of her. She had been quick to respond to Carl's emergency and had handled it with obvious competence.

Stefan ignored his lunch and asked me, "So, how are you going to find the killer?"

Whispering was only going to draw attention to our discussion, so I spoke in a normal tone. "I'm going to let the police do their job. They're busy gathering the basic information from the crime scene, and soon they'll interview everyone who might be a witness. I'm sure they'll want to talk to both of you eventually."

"I don't have anything useful to tell them," Stefan said. "I didn't see anything. Right after Sunny left, I went to find Gil. I've got information on a quilt she might be interested in acquiring. I thought she'd be in her office, but she must have been downstairs somewhere."

Detective Ohlsen would undoubtedly find it interesting that Stefan had been outside the boardroom at the time of the murder. As long as he hadn't left the museum though, the interior security cameras ought to provide him with an alibi, just as they would for Gil. In fact, they might be able to alibi each other. "Did you ever find Gil?"

Stefan shook his head. "I got distracted. I visited the restroom and then remembered there was something I wanted to check in the archives. Gil gave me a key card, so I can go there any time the museum is open. I only meant to take a quick look at the handwoven blankets, but once I started studying the collection, I lost track of time. I'd probably still be there if Sunny hadn't started screaming."

"Time always gets away from me in the archives too," I said lightly, hiding my concern that Stefan didn't have an alibi.

"I should have been with Sunny," he said. "I meant to meet her in the parking lot and help her bring in the batting. If I'd been there, maybe none of this would have happened. The kid might still be alive, and even if I hadn't prevented the murder, at least I could have given Sunny an alibi."

"It's not your fault," Sunny said briskly. "I didn't need help, or I would have asked. I think whatever happened to that poor young man, it was over before I parked my car. I didn't see anyone else the entire time I was looking for a parking space or even afterwards, at least not until Keely and Matt came running out of the building."

That reminded me of something I'd wondered about. "How did you find the body anyway? That spot is pretty isolated."

"Bad timing," Sunny said. "If I'd parked anywhere else, I never would have seen him. I really didn't want to park way back there. No one ever does, because it's kinda dark and creepy there, with just the big blank brick wall of the building—that's sort of prison-like. Plus, you have to walk past the trash, which I found out today isn't actually stinky, but you'd think it would be. Anyway, someone had taken my previous parking space, and all the other spots in the lot were occupied, so I had to take the one that no one else wanted. Even so, I wouldn't have seen the body in the shadows if I hadn't noticed a cell phone in a patch of brighter light. I went over to pick it up, thinking one of the quilters had stepped outside for a smoke and then lost her phone. That's when I saw the blood." Sunny closed her eyes again and leaned against the wall.

Stefan took her hand and patted it, but he spoke to me. "What do we do now?"

"Eat your lunch."

"No, I mean, about making sure no one blames Sunny."

"Just what I said: eat your lunch. Try to relax. Detective Ohlsen will want to talk to you both. If you have any concerns at all during the questioning, you should tell them you want to talk to your lawyer first."

Sunny opened her eyes and reclaimed her hand. "Stop worrying about me. I'll be fine. Perhaps it's just as well I was the one who found him. I don't respond well to blood, but this isn't the first corpse I've seen up close. No sense in traumatizing anyone else."

"That's my Sunny. Caring more about everyone else than about herself." Stefan stared at me meaningfully. "It's going to get her into trouble someday."

"Not today," I said firmly, hoping I was right.

He turned to Sunny. "Will you be all right for a minute without me? I need to talk to Keely about something."

Sunny had opened her take-out container, and her mouth was full. She wordlessly waved Stefan off. I had a feeling she didn't need his support as much as he needed to provide it for her.

Stefan scrambled to his feet and dragged me over to the front of the room near the white board. Once we were there, he seemed to lose all of his sense of urgency. He leaned against the wall, stared down at his feet, and tugged on his bow tie.

"Well?" I said.

He straightened and abandoned his futile adjustment of the lopsided bow tie. "I want to hire you."

In the middle of a murder investigation, he needed an appraisal?

"We can talk about it later," I said, humoring him, since he was clearly worked up about something. "You can call me any time to arrange for an appraisal if you really want one, but you've got at least as good an eye for both valuation and dating a quilt as I do. You've never needed me to second-guess you before. Why now?"

"I don't need you to do an appraisal," he said earnestly. "I need you to make sure the police understand that Sunny had nothing to do with Alan's death."

"You should talk to a criminal lawyer, not me. That was never my specialty."

"I don't care what licenses you have. All I know is that if it weren't for you, the police never would have found Randall Tremain's killer, and the wrong person would have paid the price."

"That was a fluke," I said. "I'll make sure the police understand anything they need to know about the quilting community to see possible motives in this case, but that's all I can promise."

"There's got to be more you can do," Stefan said, completely undoing his bow tie this time. "They're going to find out that Sunny hated Alan Miller, and they're going to think she killed him."

I couldn't believe it was as bad as Stefan thought. "From what I've heard, Alan had a reason to hate Sunny, but not the other way around. The police don't need me to tell them that."

Stefan huffed in frustration. "I don't understand why you're so determined to avoid using your legal skills. It's bad enough that Matt wastes his potential most of the time, but why are you doing it too?"

I didn't want to talk about my less-than-voluntary decision to leave the practice of law. Besides, while I'd heard what Matt thought the problem between them was—that Stefan couldn't accept he'd been wrong in steering Matt into a career as a fashion model and therefore couldn't accept Matt's decision to quit at the peak of his career—I was curious how Stefan would explain it. "You never did say what your problem with Matt is."

"Forget about him." Stefan waved his hand as if brushing away an irritating fly. "He gets enough attention on his own. We need to focus on protecting Sunny. She was furious with Alan for stalking her at the hospital. He couldn't accept being turned down for a job, especially when he found out no one else had been hired. She lost her temper one night when she found him lurking out near her car in the parking lot. She shouted at him, threatening to have him taken care of permanently. She only meant she'd get a restraining order, but it won't look good if it comes out. And it will. Apparently several of her friends at the hospital overheard her shouting, and they've been teasing her about it. They'd never seen her lose her temper before."

Now I could see why Stefan was so worried. If Alan had confronted Sunny today while she was getting her packages out of the car, it might have triggered something of a flashback to what had happened in the hospital parking lot. Sunny could have felt like she was being cornered and lashed out in what she thought was self-defense. Or, to put a less sympathetic spin on it, she could have seen it as an opportunity to get rid of someone who'd been tormenting her.

My hesitation seemed to push Stefan over the edge. "Please," he begged. "I don't care what it costs. Just make sure Sunny isn't blamed for this. I can't let anything happen to her."

The sensible, logical thing for me to do was to tell Stefan I couldn't help him. There was an irrational part of me though, the part that I shared with many successful trial lawyers, that insisted I was, in fact, the right person to help Stefan, perhaps the only person who could help him.

I wasn't a criminal lawyer, but I had solid negotiation skills, and I knew some of the potential suspects better than the police did. The only problem with allowing Stefan to depend on me was the risk that I'd pass out at an inconvenient moment. Ever since my diagnosis, I'd experienced recurring nightmares that started out pleasantly enough with me presenting a case in court, confident I could convince the jury of my client's position, only to experience the warning signs of a syncope event. It was too late to withdraw from the case and too late to do anything to remain conscious. No matter what happened, I knew that the client was going to pay for my failure and I would be left with overwhelming guilt.

The dreams were bad enough; I didn't need to reenact them in real life by making promises I couldn't keep. "I'll do what little I can to keep the police from heading down the wrong path. But you've got to promise me you'll hire a good defense lawyer as soon as we're allowed to leave."

"Thank you." Stefan gave me a quick hug. "Sorry. Gotta run. Sunny's trying to stand up, and I need to make sure she's steady on her feet. I'll tell her you'll take care of everything."

He trotted across the room, sliding occasionally on his overly long pants hems, before I could stop him and explain again just how little I could do.

The sense of impending failure didn't feel any better in real life than it did in my nightmares.

CHAPTER TEN

———

The volunteers who'd already given their contact information to the police were huddled as far away from the interview desk as they could get, at the end of the conference table nearest the exit, standing there and nibbling on their lunches. Even the reportedly fabulous pot stickers didn't seem to be cheering them up.

Dee and Emma were being interviewed together by Fred, which had to be against the rules, but he had enough sense to know when to bend the rules a bit. After the fiasco of Emma's wrongful arrest a few months ago, there was no way Dee would have let Emma be questioned alone, even for something as simple as contact information. Dee had a tendency to get whatever she wanted, and she didn't care about making a scene to get it. In fact, I sometimes thought the prospect of making a scene was what would keep her alive well into her hundreds.

I headed for the conference table to get my lunch, still keeping an eye on Fred's interactions with Dee and Emma. I found the take-out container with my name on it and peered inside. It looked good, although it had cooled to room temperature. I ate one of the pot stickers anyway, curious to see if it lived up to its reputation. Even cold, I could taste why Jayne was so enthusiastic about them.

After a minute or two, Dee and Emma got up and returned to their sewing machines. Jayne Connors was giving her contact information to Fred now. I could hear her shrill voice all the way across the room, piercing the background music and the subdued conversation of the other quilters.

Fred began his interview with what was probably a simple request for Jayne's name and contact information. I could only guess at his words; his deep voice wasn't pitched to be heard much beyond the desk where he was working. Jayne's response, however, came across clearly, thanks to her shrill tone. She gave her name as Jenny Smith and then rattled off a street that I didn't recognize, along with a phone number that didn't have a Danger Cove exchange.

I finished about half of my cold lunch and then tossed the rest in the trash container at the other end of the conference table. I looked up to see Meg returning from another bathroom trip. She went over to chat with Jayne, who'd finished her interview.

Right behind Meg, Faria came through the entrance, not looking particularly chastened by his conversation with Detective Ohlsen. That was just as well, since he was heading in my direction.

"Still haven't solved it?" Faria said with what he apparently thought was a light, teasing tone but came across as unbearably smug.

"I haven't really tried to solve it." I'd talked with some potential witnesses and mulled over their responses, but that was only a small part of what a real investigator would do. "It's not my job."

"That's right," he said as if he'd caught me in some sort of gaffe. "Your job is to tear down everyone else's work, making it impossible for us to get the bad guys off the street."

I'd heard that sort of thing about lawyers so often that it didn't bother me. Which was just as well, now that I couldn't handle stress very well. "That's one way of looking at it."

"You won't be able to mess up our case this time," Faria said. "It's obvious what happened here. I just saw the criminal history record on the victim. He's got prior arrests, all drug related. No convictions, but where there's smoke, there's fire. That must have been why he got killed. A drug deal gone bad."

"That's one theory," I said lightly.

"It's not like I'm happy about it," Faria said. "I wish there was another theory that made any sense. A drug deal gone bad like this, well, you know how it is. It usually ends as a cold case. I was really hoping there'd be something I could do to prove how useful I can be, but there's nothing to really investigate in this type of case."

"Just because the victim had a substance abuse problem, that doesn't mean he was killed in a drug deal."

"What else could it be?" Faria said. "Young guy with a habit gets knifed in a back alley. That seems pretty cut and dried to me."

"I wouldn't exactly describe the grounds of the museum as a back alley. This section of town has always seemed quite safe to me."

"The definition of back alleys has expanded. They can be anywhere the dealers are. Dealers and their clients take legitimate cell phone apps and twist them for use in coordinating drug deals. The victim could have ordered a drug delivery while he was standing right next to you, and you'd never have guessed what he was up to."

Alan had definitely used his phone shortly before his death. He'd said it was to call for a ride home, but since he'd had to go outside to get service, I hadn't actually heard the conversation. Could Alan have been ordering take-out narcotics, much like I'd ordered take-out food?

I hated to give Faria even that much benefit of the doubt. There had to be another explanation for what had happened to Alan. I just wished I had another theory to offer, but it was hard to imagine a killer lurking outside this museum or, really, anywhere on Danger Cove's Main Street.

Unless the killer was a thief, like Gil had suggested, and Alan had put up a struggle when someone tried to take his grandmother's quilt. I hadn't stopped to think about what had happened to the quilt until just now, but it hadn't been anywhere near his body. Maybe, as Dee and Emma believed, it had been the motive for the murder, and the killer had taken it.

"Did you see a quilt anywhere in the parking lot? White background, mostly green patches, with some red ones?" Then I remembered Alan had put it in a box before leaving. A thief might have thought there was something valuable in it. "Or perhaps a box big enough for a bed-sized quilt to fit in?"

"I have more important things to do than keep track of someone's blankie."

I was used to Faria's disdain for anything he didn't understand. Money he understood, but I couldn't honestly say that the quilt had enough financial value to make him pay attention. "It just seems odd that it wasn't right next to him. I know for a fact that Alan Miller was carrying a quilt when he left here, and he wouldn't have let it go without a struggle. It should have been near the body."

"Are you saying it was valuable?" Faria perked up. "Worth killing for?"

"No quilt is truly worth killing for, and this one isn't even worth much money. It does have a great deal of sentimental value though, and that type of emotional attachment can make a person go to seemingly irrational lengths to protect his possessions. Could you take me to talk to Detective Ohlsen? The fact that the quilt's missing might not be important, but if it is…" I trailed off, hoping Faria would leap on the possibility that he could be responsible for bringing a key piece of evidence to the detective's attention.

I could see him weighing what would get him more respect at the next crime scene: conveying my message or protecting his boss from my interference. Finally, Faria shook his head. "It's just a stupid blanket. Probably just blew away."

A quilt, either loose or in a box, wouldn't blow away in anything less than gale-force winds, and the day had been sunny and mild with air as calm as it ever got this close to the coast. "Doesn't it make you curious? I'd want to know if something was missing from the crime scene, no matter how small it was."

"Maybe." He shrugged. "I'll tell Bud when I see him, but there's no rush."

Behind me, I heard Matt laughing with his groupies. He had gotten a much better look at the crime scene than I had, so he might know if the quilt had been there and I'd just missed seeing it.

I waved at Matt to get his attention, and then called him over to where Faria and I stood at the conference table. Matt made his excuses and sauntered over.

"I know you're irritated with me about something," Matt said, "but was it so bad that you're going to turn me over to the cops?"

"Not yet," I said. "I need to know something. Did you see Alan's quilt anywhere near his body?"

Matt shook his head. "There was nothing around him except the trash enclosure, asphalt, and blood. Oh, and a cell phone."

"See?" I said to Faria. "The quilt is definitely missing. The killer must have taken it. If you find the quilt, you'll find the killer. I can even give you a picture of it from this morning's appraisal."

Faria snorted. "You want us to put out a BOLO for a *quilt*?"

"Why not?" Matt said. "Sounds like a good plan to me. When you know what to look for, quilts are pretty distinctive, like fingerprints. Plus, if the killer did take it, it's probably got blood on it that would match Alan's."

"I guess." Faria reached for his radio. "Give me a minute to arrange for someone to take my place up here, and I'll take Keely to see Ohlsen."

* * *

Matt insisted on joining us, so Richie Faria escorted both of us out to the steps at the rear of the building. Across the parking lot, Detective Ohlsen was seated on the top of the picnic table with his feet on the bench, staring at the fence past where the body had been found.

After telling the officer at the door to make sure we stayed put, Faria continued on over to the picnic table. He stood in the military at-ease position, bouncing restlessly on his toes, while he waited for the detective to acknowledge him.

If Matt and I could convince the detective that the missing quilt was important, he was more than capable of pursuing the lead. Bud Ohlsen was smart, persistent, and dedicated to nailing the right suspect, not just the most convenient one. Still, he'd barely skimmed the surface of the quilting community during the Randall Tremain investigation, so it was as if he didn't speak the same language as the people he was interviewing.

While we waited, I took in the details of the property behind the museum building. The back portion of the lot was relatively small, only about thirty feet wider than the building itself, and about a hundred feet deep. The entire space was paved, providing parking and access to the loading dock between the back door and the trash enclosure, beyond which Alan's body had been found. The far corner where Sunny's car was parked really did look a bit creepy, with overhanging tree branches and the eight-foot-high solid plank fence adding to the gloom back there. All I could see beyond the side fence was the brick wall of the second floor of a building, and beyond the back fence were some trees and the rooftops of the buildings on the next street over.

As a native of Danger Cove, Matt knew the town and the surrounding properties better than I did, so I asked him, "Do you think the killer could have escaped by climbing the fence?"

"Not unless he was a serious athlete. He'd have had to jump from the top of the fence to the roof of the next building over. There's no real alley in between, just three or four inches of empty space. Out back, there's a second fence a couple of feet over from the museum's, and the space in between is full of brambles and weedy trees." Matt turned in a half circle, inspecting the perimeter of the property. "He couldn't have gone through the loading dock, since I know it's kept locked when it's not in use. That leaves only the driveway and this door into the museum."

"Sunny would have seen anyone leaving by way of the driveway," I said. "Alan told me his friend wasn't going to be here for at least thirty or forty minutes, and that's about how long he'd been gone before Sunny found him. If the friend killed him, it would have required *Mission: Impossible*-type, split-second timing for him to lure Alan over behind the trash enclosure, commit the murder, and then leave before Sunny drove into the lot. That kind of timing and luck just doesn't happen in real life."

"We don't know how long he was dead before she found him. If it happened right after he left, it could have been anyone." Matt turned to look up at the second floor of the museum, as if he could see inside it. "But if it happened right before he was found, the odds are that the killer is upstairs in the boardroom. He couldn't have gotten into the museum from back here without setting off alarms, and if he left by the driveway, Sunny would have seen him."

I didn't want to believe it, but Matt was right. People had been coming and going from the boardroom all day, so no one would have noticed if someone had followed Alan out to the parking lot. Then afterward, the killer could have slipped into the back hallway where he or, given the gender of virtually all of the participants in today's event, she could have unobtrusively joined the crowd when everyone came down the stairs to see what the screaming was about. The presence of a stranger in the hallway would have been noticed and remembered, but no one would have paid any attention to someone who was already part of the quilting community.

"If you're right, Sunny might have seen the killer without even realizing it. Witnesses tend to remember only things that are out of place or unexpected, while more commonplace things and people barely register. A quilter going to a quilting event wouldn't be memorable."

Matt glanced across the parking lot where Faria was still waiting for Ohlsen to acknowledge him. "Do you think Ohlsen will be able to get Sunny to remember if she saw anyone?"

"It's possible," I said. "He just has to guide her through what she saw, step by step, reminding her not to skip any detail, no matter how insignificant it seems to her."

"Let's hope she remembers, then, and the case is solved right away." Matt patted five of the pockets in his cargo pants before remembering his phone had been confiscated. He glanced at my watch. "I'm already late for my meeting, but if we're not stuck here all day, I'll still have time to reschedule it for this evening, before everyone leaves town. We'll probably have to go somewhere other than the Smugglers' Tavern though. It gets busy on Saturday nights, too noisy for a meeting."

"It might not be that quick and easy to get buried information from Sunny," I said. "Sometimes the person doing the questioning assumes he knows what the witness is going to say, and he doesn't listen carefully enough to notice when something unexpected is mentioned. Ohlsen might assume that all quilters are sweet little old ladies who wouldn't hurt anyone.

If Sunny told him she saw one of the quilters as she drove through the parking lot, he might discount it, just the way Sunny herself would have done."

"Or she might not have seen anyone. What then?"

"If Ohlsen collects enough information about who was where when, he might be able to figure out who was missing from the boardroom between the time Alan left and the first of Sunny's screams."

"I was keeping an eye on Dee and Emma, trying to get a chance to talk to them," Matt said, "so I know they didn't do it. And I know you were there that whole time."

"I wonder if Elizabeth Ashby might have seen something useful," I said. "She was here this morning and left around the same time as Alan. Otherwise, there are just too many possibilities to count on a quick resolution."

Detective Ohlsen finally snapped out of his reverie enough to notice Faria. His voice carried across the parking lot. "What are you doing here? I thought you were keeping an eye on the witnesses upstairs."

"I've got some information for you, sir," Faria said, unfazed. "You remember Keely Fairchild, don't you?"

"I never forget a suspect," Ohlsen said, glaring in my direction. "And I never invite them into my crime scenes to contaminate the evidence."

"Keely's not a suspect this time," Faria said. "She's got a dozen alibi witnesses. The guy with her, Matt Viera, has even more witnesses. As far as I can tell, every single woman in the room knew exactly where he was for every single minute of the morning."

Ohlsen resumed his thoughtful study of the fence beyond the crime scene as if he hadn't even heard what Faria said. The air was getting chilly, and I was tempted to go inside and let Faria come get us if the detective ever agreed to listen to what Matt and I had to say. The cold pot stickers hadn't settled well in my stomach, or maybe it was anxiety over the day's tragic events that was affecting my digestion. I had to stay calm and keep the nausea from escalating into dizziness or worse, a syncope event. I couldn't pass out now, not before I'd alerted the detective to the missing quilt so he'd know it was connected to the murder if he found it stashed somewhere.

Detective Ohlsen pushed away from the picnic table and, ignoring Faria trailing behind him, came over to say, "I don't care if you've both got a hundred witnesses saying you never left the room from the time you arrived until the screams started. That doesn't mean you belong in my crime scene. If you've got something to tell me, we can do it somewhere you won't get in the way of the forensics team."

Ohlsen led us away from the crime scene, around the corner of the building, and all the way to the front entrance of the museum, where another uniformed officer was stationed to turn away visitors.

Detective Ohlsen stopped and turned to glare at us. "Well? What is it that you two think we're missing?" His tone let me know he wasn't happy about civilian interference.

"You're missing a quilt," I said.

That got Ohlsen's attention. His eyebrows went up. "The museum was robbed? Why didn't the director tell me this before? You think the victim stole a quilt before he was killed?"

"Sorry," I said. "I wasn't clear. Nothing's been taken from the museum. I'm talking about a quilt that belonged to the family of the young man who was killed. He brought it to me for an appraisal this morning, and he was carrying it when he left. Matt and I were the first to arrive at the crime scene after Sunny screamed, and we didn't see it there. Someone must have taken it. Possibly the killer."

"Is it valuable?"

"Not particularly." I was getting tired of everyone thinking that was all that mattered, but it wouldn't do any good to snap at the detective. "At least not in financial terms. It meant a lot to its owner, the grandmother of the victim. I think Alan cared about it too, at least enough to get it appraised and pay the fee. He wouldn't have just left it behind somewhere."

"Can you describe it well enough for my team to search for it?"

"Better than that," I said. "I can email you a picture from the appraisal, if you'll let me get my phone back from Fred. The quilt may be inside a box, and one of the women upstairs might be able to tell you if there was anything written on the outside."

"If the quilt is on the museum grounds, my team will find it. Not sure what good it will do though. Whoever killed the guy probably took the quilt, and it's long gone now. Might have thought it was more valuable than it is."

"I doubt it," I said. "People tend to discount the value of quilts because they've seen mass-produced quilts in chain stores for less than the cost of the materials for a handmade quilt. They're shocked when they hear what masterpiece quilts are worth."

Ohlsen shrugged. "Some addicts would be happy if they could sell it for twenty bucks. Or maybe the killer just liked it. My wife keeps saying she wants to learn to quilt, and she's shown me some pictures of what she wants to make. They're kind of pretty, if you like that sort of thing."

Matt spoke up. "My sources tell me the victim had a history of shoplifting, or at least being suspected of it. Anyone who knew that and saw him leaving the museum with a box might well think he'd stolen something valuable."

Detective Ohlsen nodded reluctantly. "It's a theory. Okay, I'll tell Fred to let Ms. Fairchild use her phone to send me the picture. If the quilt's not on the premises, we'll get the picture out more broadly to alert the beat cops to watch for it."

"And you'll consider the possibility that Alan was killed because of the quilt, not some other reason?"

Ohlsen frowned. "You really think that's what happened?"

"I don't know, but the quilt guild's president is convinced of it." I could see the skepticism written all over Ohlsen's face. "It's not as far-fetched as you might think. From what I've heard, Alan was never involved in anything violent until he came here with his quilt. And now the quilt is missing, and he's dead. That timing can't be a coincidence."

"It's not evidence either," Ohlsen said. "Which you, of all people, should know, Counselor."

"Evidence only comes to light if you're looking for it."

"I guess it won't hurt to keep our eyes open," Detective Ohlsen said, herding us back in the direction of the parking lot.

"Right now, I need to get to where the real evidence is most likely to be found. Can I trust you two to go straight back upstairs without sending an escort? I need all the help I can get down here. Even Faria's."

I couldn't answer for Matt, but I was as anxious to get back to the boardroom as Ohlsen was to send me there. So far, Dee and Emma had stayed out of trouble, but there was no telling what they might do if the situation dragged on for too long. Plus, I wasn't sure what Stefan might do if he thought I'd abandoned him and the search for evidence to clear his girlfriend. "I'll go straight upstairs to check in with Fred and send you the quilt picture. If you have any questions about it, I'll be in the boardroom."

"Me too," Matt said. "I'm always happy to hang out wherever Keely is."

Trust Matt to flirt even during a criminal investigation. It wasn't personal though, just a habit, like wearing cargo pants and never putting anything back in the same pocket it came from.

Detective Ohlsen walked with us toward the back entrance so we could rejoin the rest of the witnesses upstairs. "Just stay away from my crime scene."

"Of course." I wasn't particularly interested in seeing any more of the bloody evidence of a young man's death or the unadorned brick expanse of the back wall of the museum. There really wasn't anything else I could learn from the scene of the crime without first spending a couple of years getting trained in forensics.

The three of us had almost reached the museum's back entrance when a pudgy, middle-aged woman in coveralls came rushing over with an evidence bag in her gloved hands. "Sorry to interrupt, sir, but you wanted to know right away if we found anything unusual."

CHAPTER ELEVEN

———

Detective Ohlsen peered at the clear plastic bag. "What is it?"

"That's what's unusual about it," the tech said. "We have no idea."

Detective Ohlsen took the bag and raised it to eye level, inadvertently giving me a clear view of it. To a non-quilter, it would look like a crumpled Band-Aid that had once been wrapped into a cone shape around a fingertip, except it was made of well-worn leather. Its jagged edges and uneven stitches in the one seam suggested it was handmade and not commercially produced, intended to protect its wearer from the pricks of literal pins and needles.

Behind me, Matt nudged my back. I looked over my shoulder at him, and he mouthed, "Tell him."

If it were Richie Faria peering at the evidence, I wouldn't have volunteered any information, but Detective Ohlsen would listen respectfully. He might not understand, but he would at least file the information away for the next time he had a moment or ten to contemplate the case. It probably wouldn't help solve the case, but I'd feel better if Ohlsen at least knew the latest bit of evidence probably belonged to a quilter.

"Detective?" I said. "Perhaps I could help with this one little issue."

He started, as if he'd forgotten I was nearby. "You know what this thing is?"

"I think so. Do you mind if I take a closer look?"

Ohlsen held the bag in front of me, giving me a chance to study the little lump of leather. I'd never actually used a thimble like this myself, but I'd seen them in a few videos during my certification training and in person once at a quilt show. This one was an extremely simple version, just two fingertip-shaped pieces of leather about an inch and a half long, sewn together along the sides and top, leaving the bottom open. The leather was pocked with needle marks, and what had originally been flat pieces of leather had stretched around the curves of the wearer's finger.

"It's a type of thimble." I thought Matt had recognized what it was too, and unlike me, he probably knew how to use it. "Matt might be able to explain better than I can, if you want to know more."

"It's mostly used while hand quilting," Matt said. "Not on the upper hand for pushing the needle through the quilt but on the hand underneath the quilt, for deflecting the needle, so they don't prick their fingers bloody."

Detective Ohlsen sighed and handed the evidence bag back to the disappointed tech. "I suppose you even know who it belongs to, and you're going to tell me it proves the thimble's owner killed the young man."

"It's worth looking into," I said. "I know it's just circumstantial, but it might place its owner at the scene of the crime."

"Or not," Ohlsen said. "I'll have it checked for trace evidence, but I'm not counting on getting anything useful. The weather's been dry, so it could have been here for a few days. Probably nothing to do with the crime at all."

The museum brought in a textile conservator occasionally, and she had been here earlier this week, so maybe Ohlsen was right. Still, as far as I knew, the thimble was the only lead the police had. "It wouldn't be hard to figure out if it belongs to someone upstairs."

"What's the point?" Ohlsen said. "It wouldn't take a genius defense attorney to point out that it could have been dropped out here on the way into the museum this morning. You know as well as I do that a jury wouldn't have to deliberate for more than two minutes if the only thing that connected the defendant to the crime was a thimble."

"The thimble alone might not be enough for a conviction," I said, "but it might lead to other evidence if you know who it belongs to. If there's an innocent explanation for its being at the crime scene, whoever lost it will be anxious to get it back. From what I've been told, a well-broken-in thimble is the secret to heirloom-quality quilting. And if the owner doesn't claim it, that would suggest she knows it would connect her to the murder. The thimble alone might not be persuasive evidence, but lying about owning it would certainly make me suspicious. And it wouldn't be all that hard to prove who owns it. Just ask everyone to try it on. It's been well used, so over time the oils and sweat from the quilter's skin saturated the leather, causing it to shape itself around the finger until it fit her as uniquely as Cinderella's glass slipper fit her foot."

Ohlsen shook his head. "Before I start telling my forensics team that they're going to reenact a fairy tale, I'd have to be sure there's a reason to suspect that the thimble is related to the crime. For now, I'm just going to have it cataloged. Once the case is closed, I'll arrange for it to be delivered to the quilt guild to be returned to its owner. Same for the missing quilt if we find it."

I couldn't always tell what Ohlsen was thinking, but it was pretty clear I hadn't swayed him from his original theory of a falling-out among delinquents. There wasn't anything more I could say, especially since I wasn't entirely sure myself that his theory was wrong. It was just a hunch based on the missing quilt and the discovery of the thimble.

I glanced at Matt, and I thought he was debating whether to push the issue with Ohlsen. Not a good idea. We'd done our duty as upstanding citizens, and the detective had declined to pursue the lead we'd given him. On the other hand, he hadn't forbidden us from finding out more about the thimble ourselves.

Matt opened his mouth to speak, and I linked my arm with his, startling him into silence as I tugged him toward the door to the museum. "I'm sure the quilter who lost the thimble will appreciate your caring for it. Meanwhile, we'd better get back to the boardroom and leave you to your work, Detective."

Matt waited until we were out of hearing range of the officer guarding the back door before whispering, "You know as well as I do that the thimble is important. I never would have expected you to give up that easily."

"I didn't give up," I said. "I retreated to fight another day. Now we can ask around quietly to see who might have lost the thimble. We might be able to catch the killer off guard and get an answer, while Ohlsen would just get a demand to talk to a lawyer."

* * *

Matt was waylaid by his groupies as soon as we walked through the door to the boardroom. He gave me a pleading look, but there was no way I was getting between him and his admirers, least of all when they were armed with rotary cutters and seam rippers. Besides, it was a perfect opportunity for him to find out if any of them had lost a thimble.

Matt accepted his fate and allowed himself to be dragged over to the cutting table, although work had mostly been suspended with the arrival of lunch. I searched the room for Fred, so I could reclaim my phone and send Detective Ohlsen a picture of the missing quilt.

Everything felt so much different now compared to when I'd arrived this morning. Gil had been singing a fun pop song, Meg McLaughlin had been basking in the glow of the volunteers' admiration of her, and all the workstations had one or two people enthusiastically doing their part of the process.

Now, Gil was slumped in one of the chairs along the wall, all by herself, quietly singing "Peace on Earth" with a look on her face that suggested she felt none of the hope expressed in the lyrics. Stefan and Sunny were still huddled in the back corner of the room. Meg was nowhere to be seen. Trudy wandered from workstation to station, trying to keep busy, but no one had any work for her.

I found Fred at the back desk where I'd done the appraisals earlier. He had just finished collecting everyone's names and contact information, so he was free to go get my phone from wherever he'd stashed all of them.

While I waited for him to return, I went to check on Dee and Emma. They were still at the same table in the back of the room, but they'd stopped working, like almost everyone else, and were leaning against the back of their chairs instead of hunching forward over the sewing machine beds. Emma had her arms crossed over her chest and glanced at the doors every few seconds. I suspected she was looking for Meg and wondering why she wasn't in the boardroom, taking care of keeping everyone motivated. Emma certainly wouldn't have let people drift away from their work. Jayne was the only person getting anything done. She was standing at one end of the conference table with her back to the room. Apparently she was so immersed in what she was doing—layering each completed block with batting and a backing—that she hadn't noticed everyone else was slacking off.

A tall female officer I didn't recognize came inside to stand near the entrance. Unlike Faria, she didn't seem to have any immediate aspirations to becoming a detective or a stoic Buckingham Palace guard and seemed content to simply remain in the background, not bothering anyone, but ready in case of any emergency.

Dee caught the direction of my gaze and asked, "Well? Are the police being reasonable?"

"Not really, if by reasonable you mean they're zeroing in on one of the guild members as the killer." I leaned against the corner of the table. No way was I sitting down where I might be expected to use a sewing machine. "Shouldn't you be happy that none of your friends are being considered suspects?"

"I would if I were certain none of them killed that young man," Dee said. "It would be nice to think that quilters never commit crimes, but I'm not either senile or naive. Most of us are decent law-abiding citizens, but there's always a bad apple or two. It's not like we run criminal background checks before admitting people into our guild."

"Maybe we should." Emma straightened and lowered her hands to her lap. "We don't always know people as well as we think we do. Just look at what happened at the Smugglers' Tavern. And at the Painted Lady that Alex Jordan was renovating. Even, and I still can't quite believe it, at the Cinnamon Sugar Bakery. You just never know when someone will snap. Especially this time of year. The holidays can be stressful for quilters who are trying to finish quilts for everyone on their Christmas list. And stress can make people do things they wouldn't otherwise."

I knew that only too well. "I didn't notice anyone who looked frazzled this morning. Anyone with quilts to finish for Christmas is probably too busy to leave her sewing room."

Dee did a scan of the room and its occupants before finally nodding. "You're right. It's mostly beginners who plan to do too much, and except for Trudy, I'm not seeing any real novices here."

"Janiece Jordan and her friends are making Christmas quilts together, and some of them aren't anywhere close to finishing them," Emma said. "That's why they're not here today."

I hadn't met Janiece, but her granddaughter, Alex, had been the contractor who transformed a small bank branch building into my residence.

"They should be here today," Dee said irritably. "There's no need to rush a holiday quilt. There's always next year. In fact, back when Meg still lived in Danger Cove, she made an heirloom-quality Christmas quilt. She did it in stages, just a little bit each December, so it took about ten years to finish."

"I never saw the quilt, but I heard about it from Jayne." Emma picked up the two remaining pieces of fabric next to her sewing machine. "Because of course Jayne had to do the same thing with her own Christmas quilt. She probably could have finished it in half the time, but she made sure it would take the full ten years, as if there was some magic to that number."

Dee pursed her lips disapprovingly. "I've been telling Jayne for years that her quilts could easily eclipse her mentor's if only she'd stop religiously copying everything Meg does. That slavish devotion really limits Jayne. But she won't listen to me. Only to Meg."

That might change soon, judging by the way Emma had abandoned her pieces of fabric and was now staring at Jayne appraisingly. We really didn't need another confrontation today, least of all between two such strong-minded women as Emma and Jayne.

To distract Emma, I said, "I wonder what the history was behind Alan's Tree of Life quilt. It looked like it had been used hard, not reserved for the holidays."

"Mmm," Emma said as she continued to stare at Jayne.

"Oh, not everyone treats their quilts like fine art, to be locked away and untouched most of the year," Dee said. "I use all of my quilts or give them away, and if they get a bit worn or stained, it doesn't really matter to me. It's the process of making them that I love, not owning them. Emma's a bit more sentimental about some of them than I am."

"Only a little," Emma said, finally abandoning her close watch on Jayne. "We quilt all the time, so it's not associated with specific memories. It's different for people who make their holiday quilts part of a family tradition, as meaningful as decorating the Christmas tree or hanging stockings. Eventually, just looking at the quilt or feeling its warm weight wrapped around them can bring back years of family memories."

Dee turned to Emma. "Do you remember a few years ago when one of our guild members lost her house in a fire on Christmas Eve?" Dee turned back to me. "No one was hurt, fortunately, but they lost everything they owned. I think they were more upset about losing their Christmas quilts than losing their kids' baby pictures."

"The guild got together and reproduced their favorite quilt, and the family was grateful," Emma told me, "but you could tell it just wasn't the same for them."

"The reproduction will be part of new traditions for the family," Dee said briskly, clearly done with any hint of sentimentality. "I'm more concerned with the police investigation into Alan's murder. Did they tell you anything useful?"

"Not really," I said. "I did convince them to look for Alan's missing Tree of Life quilt, so it wasn't a total waste of my time. Fred's getting my camera so I can send Detective Ohlsen a picture from this morning's appraisal."

Dee snorted. "Like they'll really look for it. Quilts are stolen all the time, and they hardly ever get found."

I'd heard that before from Stefan, who'd had a few quilts stolen from his gallery over the years and had never recovered any of them. "It must be particularly devastating when a Christmas quilt is stolen."

"It is," Dee said. "And usually the police don't do anything more than take a report. I remember quite a few years ago—at least twenty, long before I met Emma, so she wouldn't remember—a beloved Christmas quilt was stolen right here in Danger Cove. Caused quite a ripple in the community, and it was never found. Alan's probably won't be either."

"Ohlsen promised he'd look for it. If anyone can track it down, he can." I realized this was a perfect opening to ask about the ownership of the thimble without giving away its importance. "He also promised to return a leather thimble that was found in the parking lot, once it's released from evidence. I thought maybe you'd have an idea of who might have lost it."

Dee looked at Emma, and they both shook their heads. Dee said, "I'm afraid I couldn't even tell you who in the guild wears a leather thimble. They're usually used on the bottom hand, out of sight. A few people wear them in place of metal thimbles on the top hand, but I can't think of any current guild members who do that."

"Or you could check with Trudy." Emma nodded at where Trudy was loitering near the cutting table in the front of the room. "She's fascinated by all the varieties of thimbles. Take a look at her charm bracelet. It's got more than a dozen types of thimbles on it. She even had reproductions of some of the more unusual styles custom made for her by a silversmith. If you can find one on her bracelet that looks like the one the cops found, she might know who it belongs to."

"There's no rush. I'll ask her later." Questioning Trudy would have to be done carefully to avoid focusing too much attention on the thimble. I had a better chance of getting honest answers if no one was tipped off to the possibility that it might connect them to the murder. "Perhaps you could help me with something else for now. I noticed on my way over here that the basket of finished ornaments is overflowing. Transferring them into a storage box is about the only thing I'm actually qualified to do. Is there a box somewhere to hold them? I'd rather not get Jayne involved."

"It's always best not to get Jayne involved," Dee said.

"I've got some boxes in my car," Emma said, prepared as always, "but I'd have to go past Jayne and get a police escort to get them."

"I could distract Jayne while you made your escape," Dee said. "I've always wanted to see if she'd dare to tell me I don't know how to quilt. I could use the wrong seam allowance and then go ask her why the block came out smaller than the others."

"If you brought a subpar block to Jayne, she'd know you were provoking her."

"But think how crazy that would make her, knowing that I could do better and was only making a mess to taunt her," Dee said with a gleeful smile. "Emma would have no trouble slipping past her then."

"I think we've had enough emotional upheaval for one day."

"I suppose you're right," Dee said with obvious disappointment. "Jayne is a valued member of our guild. I need to remember that."

"You're only human." Emma patted her friend's hand. "And Jayne could irritate a saint. If she ever met one, she'd probably get into an argument over the proper way to be a good person, trying to convince him he was doing it wrong."

"Jayne's already told the police that she could investigate the murder better than they could," I said. "One of the few things I know about criminal defense work is that it never pays to argue with the police outside of court. I've heard too many stories from colleagues about clients who were on the verge of being let go with a warning until they decided to mouth off and got arrested instead."

"Sounds like something Jayne would do," Dee said. "In fact, I vaguely recall hearing she actually did something like that once. Got into an argument after being pulled over for speeding. She was adamant that she'd been within the posted limit and told the police officer he needed to check his eyesight. I don't remember how it ended, but it sounded a great deal more complicated and expensive than simply paying the ticket or filing an appeal would have been."

Perhaps that explained why Jayne had given a false name during the interview. One bad experience with the police might have led her to be extra cautious in subsequent encounters with them. Except Jayne didn't strike me as the cautious type, or even the learning-her-lesson type. Plus, lying to the police during a homicide investigation was considerably riskier than simply yelling at a trooper writing out a ticket. Why would Jayne take that sort of risk? Unless she was hiding something that would get her into more trouble than lying about her name.

"Has Jayne been a guild member for long?"

Dee looked to Emma, who supplied the details. "Longer than I have, so more than five years. She isn't from Danger Cove originally though. All I know is her ex-husband teaches at the high school, and that's why they moved here. They never had kids, and she works in retail in one of the surrounding towns, but I'm not sure which one. I try to avoid conversations with her, although I usually can't help eavesdropping. Her voice cuts through everything, but she's almost always talking about quilts, not her job or anything personal. That's probably why we tolerate her. Listening to her pontificate about a subject we enjoy is bad enough. If she went on and on about things we weren't interested in, it would be torture."

"She really is well intentioned," Dee said. "I just wish she'd relax a little. For her sake, as well as everyone else's."

I still didn't understand why Jayne would intentionally lie to the police about her identity. I hadn't caught the entirety of the conversation between Jayne and Fred, so maybe I'd misunderstood. Perhaps Jayne hadn't been identifying herself, but had been indirectly telling the officer how to do his job by giving him the name of someone she thought he should interview. That did sound like something Jayne would do. Maybe Dee or Emma would recognize the name Jayne had given.

"I'm starting to realize just how little I know about the quilt guild's members, other than you two," I said. "I was hoping to meet some of them in person today after having corresponded with them online. There's one in particular that I wanted to talk to. Her name is Jenny Smith."

After a glance at Emma, who shook her head, Dee said, "There are a couple of Jennys in the guild, but no Jenny Smith."

"I must have remembered part of the name wrong." Or heard it wrong. I was certain about the last name though. That had come through loud and clear. "Perhaps a Smith with a different first name?"

Emma shook her head. "There aren't any Smiths in the guild. You'd think there'd be at least one in a group of close to a hundred, if you count the people who occasionally come from out of town, but it's not all that common a name here."

"We could ask around for you," Dee said. "Try to figure out who it was."

"It's not that important." I noticed Meg return from her latest bathroom trip. Jayne turned around as if she had some sort of early warning system for her mentor's presence. In a moment, Jayne was going to notice that no one was doing any quilt making. "Jayne is going to start cracking the whip any minute now. I don't want to be blamed for keeping you from your work."

Emma handed two unstitched pieces of fabric to Dee. "We don't have anything left to sew after this, and no one's doing any gophering. I'll go see what I can rustle up for us to work on."

Emma left, and Dee placed the fabric squares under the sewing machine's foot. She tromped on the pedal, but I could swear the motor sounded slower and sadder than before.

CHAPTER TWELVE

———

I left Dee to her work and headed for the doors to see if Fred had found my phone, so I could claim to be doing something useful if Jayne decided to single me out for a lecture.

I had to remind myself that even though she was the one person here I wouldn't feel bad about sending to jail, there wasn't any evidence that she'd done anything criminal. She probably had a perfectly reasonable explanation for giving the cops a name that wasn't hers, something totally irrelevant to the homicide investigation and absolutely none of my business.

Unless, of course, Jayne was somehow involved in Alan Miller's murder, and that was why she'd given the police false information. Then, it was my business, if only because I felt some responsibility for what had happened to Alan. Plus, I'd promised Stefan I'd do what I could to keep Sunny from being wrongly accused of the murder, and I hadn't come up with anything solid.

The female officer stationed at the door kept a close eye on me but didn't prevent me from stepping out into the hall to look for Fred. He was near the stairwells that led down to the first floor, talking to someone on his phone. He showed me that he had my phone in his jacket pocket and then held up one finger to ask me to wait a minute. I stepped back inside the boardroom to give him some privacy. Just then, Matt said something to his groupies at the cutting table, and they wandered off, leaving him behind.

Matt beckoned me over to the deserted cutting table. "Half the people in the room look like they're attending a wake for young Mr. Miller," Matt said.

"There'd be more smiling at a wake." I nodded at where the unnamed replacement for Faria stood. "And fewer police officers."

Matt waved a greeting at the officer and asked me, "Did you find out anything about the thimble?"

"No. You?"

He shook his head. "Sorry. I asked, but the ones I talked to are all machine quilters, not hand quilters. They said Trudy might know, but I think it would be better if you asked her. I make her nervous."

Before I could answer, I saw that the intense conversation between Meg and Jayne was breaking up. Meg strode past me over to the white board and clapped her hands, proving that she could get everyone's attention without Jayne's assistance.

"You all know what a hard taskmaster I am," Meg said. "You've had a much-longer lunch break than we'd planned, and the ornaments won't make themselves. It's time for us all to get back to work now."

No one moved.

Meg continued. "Look, I know it's difficult to think about anything other than this morning's tragedy, but no one's ever said that quilting was easy, right?"

Most of the women nodded, and a few responded with a smile and a halfhearted, "Right." Even Jayne's shrill agreement barely registered.

Meg acted as if she'd received a rousing chorus of support. "That's settled then. We have plenty of supplies and nowhere to go until the police finish their work, so let's see how many ornaments we can make. I'm betting that the museum will need the biggest tree on the West Coast to fit them all. Are you with me?"

This time, Meg did get a bit more enthusiasm. It might have been because Jayne was mingling with the volunteers. She bore down on one group of women leaning against the conference table, and they promptly scurried over to take up positions at various workstations. The sound of the sewing machines began to fill the room.

Matt went over to where he and Carl had been working earlier, where he could keep a close reporter's eye on the comings and goings of everyone involved with the investigation, police and witnesses alike. Within a couple of minutes, all of the various workstations were occupied by volunteers with a renewed sense of purpose.

Trudy headed toward where Jayne had been basting the layers of the ornaments together, only to be cut off by three BFFs who didn't notice her as they took over that station. Trudy turned in a circle, searching for someplace she might be useful, and ended up standing next to me.

Before I could ask her about thimbles, Meg bustled over to us. "You can be a gopher again," Meg told Trudy. "I think Dee and Emma already have some rows that need ironing, if you could fetch them."

Asking about the thimble found at the crime scene would have to wait, if I didn't want to draw too much attention to the topic.

Trudy headed off on her mission, obviously relieved to have a purpose. Fred was still out in the hall, and I didn't want to stand around looking useless while I waited. Not with Jayne on the hunt for slackers.

I turned to Meg. "Is there anything I can do? Something that doesn't involve cutting, sewing, or ironing?"

"You can be a gopher too, once the work starts to pile up," Meg said. "Although right now, what would really help is if you'd take my place while I run to the ladies' room again. Just keep an eye out for anyone who looks confused or upset, tell them they're doing fine, and keep them calm until I get back."

"I can do that." I doubted any real supervision was necessary, since Jayne was already making a circuit of the room like an exam-room proctor, swooping down on anyone who was doing something imperfectly. Actually, that might be the real reason why Meg wanted someone to keep an eye on the room: to make sure Jayne didn't escalate the tension. "I'm good at watching other people work."

"Thanks." Meg rushed off, with the female officer following her out into the hallway.

As they left, Fred came inside, carrying my phone. He handed it to me, and I sent the picture of the Tree of Life quilt to the address Ohlsen had given me.

As I handed the phone back to Fred, I asked, "Any idea how much longer before Ohlsen will be ready to interview us and let us go home? I'm not sure how much longer everyone's renewed sense of purpose is going to last. My guess is it won't take long before people start getting restless."

"I wish I knew." Fred reached into the pocket where the bakery bag had been earlier, only to come up empty. "My wife and I were supposed to be doing some Christmas shopping today. Sally knows my schedule can be unpredictable, but she still gets irritated sometimes when I have to put in some unexpected overtime. I've got to admit the overtime pay will come in handy this time of year, but it's not like I'm happy someone got killed, just because it got me out of doing some chores and added a few bucks to my paycheck."

Jayne finished her circuit of the room and took a break from criticizing her fellow quilters by focusing on a new target: Fred. She turned her back on the room to ask him, "How much longer can it possibly take your colleagues to clear one tiny little crime scene?" Jayne's voice was shrill enough that the women at the cutting table less then ten feet away could certainly hear every word distinctly. The female officer in the hallway could probably catch the gist of Jayne's complaint too. For a woman who might be hiding a secret behind a false name, Jayne wasn't exactly keeping a low profile.

Fred was too well trained to rise to her bait. "It shouldn't be much longer, ma'am." He didn't stick around to hear her response but headed back out into the hall, leaving me as the sole audience for her rant.

"It's just so inefficient," she said. "I could have collected all the necessary information from the witnesses in half the time, without forcing a work stoppage. We'll never reach our target for completed ornaments now."

"Meg seemed confident that there will be plenty of ornaments."

Jayne snorted. "Only if she makes them herself at home after we're done here."

"As long as they get done in time for Christmas," I said, "does it really matter how or when? A young man is dead, after all. I'm sure the museum will be fine with a few less ornaments than planned."

"It's just not fair," Jayne insisted. "Why did that guy have to get killed today? He shouldn't even have been here. He wasn't a quilter, and he didn't appreciate the quilt enough to take proper care of it. I could tell that much from across the room when he spread it out on your table. Meg and I were both impressed by the design, but then we saw how tattered it was. Meg was appalled at the disrespect that had been shown to a work of art."

"Still, mistreating a quilt isn't a capital offense," I said.

"I know that," Jayne said, irritability adding to the shrillness of her tone. "But little things can tell you a lot about a person. I can tell you how another person's quilt is going to turn out just from seeing how a person treats her tools. It's the same way with understanding people. You could see that Alan didn't take care of anything he owned, not his quilt, not his clothes, not even his own body. He probably did all sorts of things that were bad for him. That's what got him killed, nothing to do with the museum or the quilters."

"Things that might seem obvious to you still need to be proven in court," I said, a bit stunned at Jayne's belief that she had deep insights into human behavior. "The police need more than speculation, and credible evidence takes time to gather. We're luckier than most crime scene witnesses. We're not stuck here with nothing to do but sit and wait. We have plenty to keep us busy."

Jayne sighed and turned around to face the room, crossing her arms over her chest. "Busy, sure. But that's not the same as productive. We're going to have to unstitch at least half of the blocks before we can use them. No one's paying proper attention to their work."

Meg hurried in from the hallway in time to catch Jayne's last words. "It doesn't matter if some of the blocks are less than perfect. We'll just pretend we intended them to be that way, like Matt does."

Jayne mellowed instantly. "That's brilliant! We could add some uneven borders to emphasize the effect. I'll go see how many blocks need that treatment."

Once she was gone, Meg said, "I'm sorry if Jayne's been irritating you. I keep hoping that with enough classroom experience she might mellow enough to be an effective teacher. She's such a brilliant quilter, and people could learn so much from her if she didn't set their nerves on edge. I can't seem to get through to her though. Probably because teaching just comes naturally to me. I get along with people as easily as she annoys them."

"Fortunately, there's room for both of you in the quilting world," I said. "Now that you're back, I'd better go do some gophering before Jayne notices that I'm not doing anything."

"And I'd better get back to soothing the feathers that Jayne has ruffled." Meg leaned in to speak in a quiet tone meant only for my ears. "Thanks for watching the room for me. One of these days I'm going to give in and wear an adult diaper during workshops so I don't have to leave so often. At least today my bladder issues turned out to be something of a blessing. I was in the ladies' room when the screaming started, and it took a couple of minutes before I could leave. By the time I got to the back door, you and that reporter had everything under control, so I didn't have to take charge. I wouldn't have known what to do at a crime scene."

"Matt is good in emergencies," I said humbly, although I was rather pleased that I'd managed not to pass out during the crisis.

Meg frowned. "It's a little odd though. I would have expected Jayne to be right there on the spot, telling everyone what to do. I didn't see her on the back steps though. I wonder where she was."

That was a good question. I'd been too busy comforting Sunny and then getting the blanket out of Matt's car to notice who was in the huddle near the back door or when each of them had arrived. Surely, if Jayne had been there, issuing orders in her shrill voice, I would have heard her. All I could remember though was the quiet hum of shocked conversation from the quilters gathered at the back door and then Carl's deep, commanding voice gathering everyone back into the building.

Had Jayne been there, shocked into silence for once? Or had she been hiding somewhere because she'd just come in from the parking lot after killing Alan, and was waiting for a chance to mingle with the rest of the quilters who'd come downstairs at the sound of the screams?

CHAPTER THIRTEEN

———

"Jayne's at it again," Meg said with a deep sigh, interrupting my thoughts. "Excuse me while I go deal with her. I swear I could manage better without an assistant."

Right after she left, before I could start on my gophering duties, Faria came through the doorway with Carl and his service dog. I was relieved to see that Rusty seemed calm, the bringsel hanging loose, confirming that his master wasn't in any medical distress. I was glad to see that Carl was better, although I would have preferred it if his return hadn't brought Faria back too.

The officer gave Carl a friendly punch in the upper arm by way of a farewell and then started toward the far end of the room. Carl seemed to relax when he caught sight of Trudy happily trotting from station to station. He swiped a stack of red-and-white fabric squares from the cutting table and then headed over to the vacant sewing machine next to Matt. Rusty curled up under the table at Carl's feet.

Meanwhile, Faria had stopped at the ironing board where Stefan and Sunny were working. They were too far away for me to hear what they were saying, and I couldn't think of an excuse to go over and join them without being obvious enough that Faria would be justified in reporting me to Detective Ohlsen. Still, from their actions, I could tell Faria was here to collect Sunny to be interviewed. She finished the piece she was ironing and set the iron down, prepared to go with Faria, but Stefan took her hand in both of his and said something to Faria.

It wasn't hard to guess that Stefan was insisting that they couldn't be separated. He nodded in my direction, probably reading more into my promise to help Sunny than I'd intended, and Faria turned to look at me before shrugging and apparently agreeing the couple didn't need to be separated yet. For once, he seemed to understand that he should leave the matter up to someone with more experience in handling anxious witnesses. As long as all Faria was doing was delivering Sunny and Stefan to Detective Ohlsen for their interview, there was nothing I could or should do to protect them.

It was actually an encouraging sign that Ohlsen was finally starting to take witness statements. We might not be stuck here much longer, and the sooner we could leave, the less traumatized the quilters would be by today's events, and the less likely they'd be to associate the museum with an unpleasant experience.

I still needed to see if anyone knew who owned the leather thimble. I'd been too distracted to ask Jayne or Meg, and in any event, they were unlikely to recognize it. Meg hadn't lived in Danger Cove for years, so she wouldn't have had many opportunities to get to know the idiosyncrasies of the local guild members. Jayne knew the local quilters, but she only noticed the things that were being done wrong. The owner of the thimble probably had solid skills, given the extensive wear that would only come from putting in the long hours of work that generally led to competence.

Carl might recognize it though, and Matt seemed to have forgotten that we were on a mission to find the thimble's owner. Matt was bent over his sewing machine, stitching at a speed that would make me dizzy if I tried to work that fast. His blocks might not have the assembly-line type of precision that Jayne and Meg insisted on, but I thought his intense concentration on the little pieces of folk art surpassed that of anyone else in the room.

I slipped into the vacant seat next to Carl. "Are you sure you should be here?"

He finished the perfect little seam he was stitching and then said, "I'm fine. I just needed to rehydrate, and then Rusty convinced the EMTs that I really didn't need to go to the hospital. It was nothing, really."

"It wasn't nothing." It felt a little surreal to be saying the exact words that my paralegal used to say to me, back when I was in denial about my syncope diagnosis. "You were unconscious. That's serious."

Carl picked up another pair of fabric squares and lined the edges up precisely. "Not this time. It's just part of living with diabetes. I've learned which things are serious and which aren't. I'm lucky to have Rusty, who can provide a second opinion. I trust him to know when I need help."

"Still, it wouldn't have hurt to get an actual medical opinion."

"In other circumstances, I might have." He glanced over his shoulder, and I had a feeling that if I followed his gaze, I would have been looking at Trudy. "It wouldn't be fair for me to be treated differently than everyone else here. I never liked it when I got special treatment because of my job, and I don't like it now when it's for other reasons."

I could understand that. I'd never liked it when people fussed over me after I passed out.

"Besides," Carl said. "I'm worried about Trudy. She was terrified while she was waiting to be interviewed by Richie Faria. I thought she might have some sort of episode herself, in fact. That's probably why I didn't notice that I wasn't feeling well until it was too late."

"Everything seems to terrify Trudy," I said. "But she's young, and she recovers quickly."

Carl nodded. "Still, someone needs to keep an eye on her. She's fine now, but she might fall apart when Bud interviews her. She got some strange notion into her head that she might be blamed for Alan's death."

"Trudy?" This time I did turn and follow his gaze to look at the timid young woman laughing at something Emma had said to her. "Why would anyone think she might be violent? She's got victim written all over her, not attacker."

"It didn't make sense to me either, but it was obvious she believed it." Carl turned back to his sewing machine and concentrated on placing the two squares on the sewing plate. He fidgeted with them until they were in exactly the right spot, which didn't seem all that different to me from where they'd started, and dropped the presser foot. "I would have asked, but then Faria called her over to his desk, and I started to feel a bit dizzy, and then, well, you were there. You probably know better than I do what happened next."

Carl had spent enough time on the police force that he had to know anyone could become violent in the right circumstances. I'd learned that lesson in the course of my legal career, and then in more personal terms during my investigation of Randall Tremain's murder. Even so, I had trouble imagining Trudy stabbing someone.

I gave Carl a reassuring grin. "You couldn't have created a better distraction for Trudy if you'd been trying to do it. When you collapsed, she forgot about being afraid of Faria so she could be brave for you."

Carl looked up from the sewing machine bed, worry lines etched across his forehead. "Did you notice how afraid she was of Alan? I saw it earlier, when he first arrived. I'd have been watching him anyway, given his history, but when I saw how scared Trudy was, I thought it might help if she knew I had her back."

"I'm sure she appreciated your presence," I said. "And that only makes it more ridiculous to think she might have killed Alan. She didn't need to do anything to him if he bothered her, not with you right here and prepared to help."

"Yeah, that's what I thought." He stepped on the pedal, keeping the needle at a much safer speed than Dee and Emma had. "I just wish I knew for sure. Maybe I should have told her not to leave this room until I got back from walking Rusty, so she wouldn't risk being alone with Alan, and then she'd have had an obvious alibi."

"Now you're being silly." I'd experienced the same sort of irrational guilt in the wake of Randall Tremain's death, as if there had to have been something I could have done differently that would have prevented the crime, even when I knew there wasn't. "It's not your fault that Alan is dead or even that Trudy doesn't have an alibi for the time of the murder. You should probably be more concerned about the fact that you don't have an alibi either."

"I'm no vigilante," Carl said. "I'm just a useless ex-cop."

"And an accomplished quilter," I said, hoping to turn the conversation to where I could ask about thimbles without raising any suspicion. "There aren't many people whose stitching can meet Meg McLaughlin's high standards."

"I like precision work. It takes my mind off other things."

"I'd love to see one of your finished quilts someday. Do you have any special style you're known for?"

"I like modern quilts, the ones with simple lines sort of reminiscent of Frank Lloyd Wright's architecture. But I like to interpret them using lots of little pieces within each of the large sections."

The "modern quilt" movement was something of a recent phenomenon in the quilting world, with simple but precise piecing that often relied on particularly fancy quilting to bring the minimalist piecing into a more complicated overall design. It gave me the perfect opportunity to ask him about thimbles.

"I can see that you do excellent piecing, but do you send the tops out to be finished, or do you also do the quilting?"

"I do it myself," he said. "I find hand quilting relaxing."

"I've never tried it," I said honestly. "It looks somewhat painful actually, pushing a tiny, sharp needle through all those layers, multiplied by several stitches on the needle each time. It has to be hard on the fingers, especially for someone like me who's never gotten used to a thimble."

"I can't use a thimble either. I tried at first, but I finally figured out the only way I can quilt is with a stab stitch." He must have seen the confusion on my face, because he explained. "It's just one stitch at a time. Push the needle through from the top of the quilt to the back, pull it all the way through underneath, and then poke it back up to the top. It can be slow, but it doesn't require as much pressure on the fingers, so there's less need for a thimble." Carl raised one hand from the table, turning his palm upward to stare at it. "It's not like I'd even notice if I inadvertently got pricked while quilting, considering how often I have to do it on purpose for testing."

Matt suddenly stopped sewing and leaned toward Carl to say in a low voice, "Heads up, guys. I think Jayne just noticed that you two aren't working."

I felt Rusty shift beneath the table, and Carl shuddered. "Jayne's worse than my old sergeant."

I pushed myself to my feet. I could either gopher or sew, and there was no way I was operating anything motorized. The paramedics surely had better things to do than to visit the museum for a third time today.

* * *

Trudy was busy in the back of the room, delivering quilt pieces from station to station, so I stayed in the front, starting at the cutting table. I hadn't had a chance earlier to see what they were doing there in any detail, and I was curious about the process.

The women had an efficient assembly line going. One person cut the red fabrics into narrow strips from selvage to selvage, then cut the strips at the appropriate intervals to create one-and-a-half-inch and two-inch squares. Another woman did the same thing with the white fabric. A third woman took the various squares and sorted them into plastic baggies that contained enough pieces in the right sizes to make a block that would eventually become an ornament.

After a couple of minutes, when a whole stack of baggies had been compiled, I took them over to the sewing machine tables and offered them to anyone who didn't already have a stack of fabric pieces to sew. Along the way, I collected any blocks that were finished except for the final ironing. When I'd distributed all the baggies, I brought the sewn blocks to where a woman I didn't know had taken over Stefan's ironing board. She gave me a stack of finished blocks to take over to yet another station at the end of the conference table, where the blocks were layered with batting and a red print for the back. The three layers were then pinned together for the quilting. I took those layered blocks to the opposite end of the conference table, where a sewing machine had been set up after lunch had been cleared away. There, the blocks were quilted. I traded the layered blocks for a stack that had been quilted and took them over to the final station in the front corner of the room. The machine there had a special foot for attaching the binding around the edge of the quilted block. An extra length of binding formed a loop for hanging it.

I gathered some more baggies filled with cut pieces and distributed them around the room. When I saw Meg was having a private word with Jayne over near the white board and wouldn't be paying attention to me, I headed for Matt's table and offered him the last of my baggies.

He shook his head. "Not my style. I cut my own pieces so I can work free form."

I turned to the next row of sewing machines behind Matt and held up the baggie. One of the women raised her hand, and I tossed it to her.

"Do you have a minute?" I asked Matt.

"I've always got time for you."

Not for the past twelve weeks he hadn't. It was too petty a complaint for me to say out loud though, given the events of today.

"It's making me nervous, how long the cops are keeping us here." I kept my voice low, although I didn't think anyone but Matt could hear me over the roar of the sewing machines. The women at the table behind us didn't seem to be paying us any attention. The people closest to us were Fred and Gil, talking in the doorway, but I couldn't make out exactly what Fred was saying or what song Gil was humming, so they weren't likely to be able to eavesdrop. "I wish I knew what Ohlsen was thinking."

"It is nerve wracking, isn't it?" He raised his hands to his cheeks, doing an exaggerated impression of Edvard Much's painting *The Scream*. "It's like we're in a manor-house mystery, locked up with all the suspects, unable to leave, while we get picked off, one by one. First Alan and then Carl."

From the other side of Matt, Carl raised one hand. "I'm still here. I didn't get picked off. I just wasn't paying enough attention to my medical condition. No one to blame except myself."

"Are you sure?" Matt turned to ask him. "You've been dealing with your diabetes for a while now, and you had some intense training with Rusty. So how come you didn't notice something was wrong before it was too late?"

Rusty poked his head out from under the table. Carl reached down to pat him. "It's okay, boy. He didn't mean it. It wasn't your fault." He told Matt, "I saw Rusty's signals, but I thought I could wait a few more minutes. He was doing his job. I was the one who messed up."

"I'm just saying the crisis seemed to happen awfully fast," Matt said. "Like it even took Rusty by surprise. Could someone have triggered the event somehow? Spiked your water bottle or something?"

Carl shrugged. "I suppose anything's possible. If there was a simple way to treat or monitor blood sugar and hydration, we wouldn't need service dogs."

"So someone *could* be trying to pick us off, one by one," Matt said triumphantly.

"But why?" I said. "What do Alan and Carl have in common that someone would target both of them?"

Matt wrinkled his nose. "See, this is why I leave crime reporting to the pros."

"I know. I know. You're just a simple arts reporter."

"Hey, that's right," Matt said, unfazed by my implied skepticism. "And in the arts, the second killing is usually to take care of loose ends from the first killing. Carl was outside near the time of the murder. Maybe he saw something incriminating."

"I wish I had seen something," Carl said morosely. "I'd have told Bud the minute he got here, and he'd have the suspect in custody by now. Except I didn't see anything. There was no one in the parking lot when Rusty and I were out there. Not even Alan Miller."

"You've seen too many movies based on Agatha Christie novels," I told Matt. "One person dying today is more than enough. And I really don't think Alan's killer was any kind of mastermind who would plot a whole series of murders. I can't see how any of this could have been planned in advance. Alan said he only heard about the event this morning, right before he came here, and apparently no one expected Carl to be here today."

Matt looked like he was going to argue with me, but I held up a hand. "And don't even think about mentioning the possibility of more victims if Stefan can hear you. He's already convinced he almost lost Sunny earlier today. He'll go into a total panic if he starts wondering whether the killer might be targeting her now because she saw something she shouldn't have."

"Maybe she did," Matt said. "Did you ask her?"

"She didn't see anything." I couldn't hide my frustration at how little we knew about what had happened. "At least not that she remembers."

"Isn't that the way it usually works?" Matt said. "The killer thinks someone saw more than she actually did."

"I'm not an expert in the mental processes of killers," I said. "What I do know is that Sunny is a lot stronger than Stefan is giving her credit for, and he's not going to let her out of his sight. So I think she's pretty safe unless the killer is prepared to take out two people simultaneously."

"Sunny's not the only one at risk," Matt said. "You and I are probably safe, just because we were both up here when the murder happened and couldn't possibly have seen anything incriminating. Everyone else is fair game."

Matt might appear laid back and less than serious, but he was also smart. I knew that he resented being dismissed as nothing but a pretty face every bit as much as I resented the way my syncope events gave people the impression that I was weak. He might just be right about someone having seen something incriminating without realizing it.

Carl had already claimed he hadn't seen anything, and he was a trained observer, so I believed him. He wasn't the only person who'd been out of the boardroom during the relevant time frame though. "I suppose Meg could have seen something on one of her trips to the ladies' room. Or Gil on her way down to the museum lobby."

Matt blinked. "Wait. Gil doesn't have an alibi? I thought she was up here all morning."

I shook my head. "There was some problem in one of the exhibit rooms. She went down to take care of it before Alan left. She was gone until after the murder. I expect the security cameras down there will exonerate her of the crime though."

"What about the cameras in the parking lot?" Matt blinked. "Wait, don't tell me. The museum got hit by the hooligans competing to knock out all the cameras in town."

"It's possible," I said, since I couldn't betray what Gil had confided to me in private. "But if so, the killer wouldn't have known the cameras were out. The museum certainly wouldn't advertise the fact. Maybe the police are right, and the killing really was just a matter of Alan's past catching up with him. If it was one of us who killed him—one of the quilters, I mean—they would have thought there was surveillance footage of the crime, and they'd have run away instead of coming inside and pretending nothing had happened."

"People live in denial all the time," Matt said. "Maybe the killer thought he'd stayed out of range of the cameras. The body was in an isolated corner of the lot, after all."

"You're determined to make me feel like I'm in a horror movie with a killer lurking around every corner, aren't you?"

"Don't worry," he said with a grin. "I'll protect you."

I almost believed him.

CHAPTER FOURTEEN

———

Trudy apparently noticed that I'd stopped gophering and came over to our table. She reached hesitantly toward the chain of five or six finished blocks that were still attached by threads to each other and to Matt's sewing machine. Without taking her eyes off the blocks, she said, "May I take these over to the ironing board for you?"

Matt used a seam ripper to disconnect the chain of blocks from the one under the sewing machine foot and then from each other, since Faria had confiscated all the scissors.

As Matt tossed each one to Trudy, she smoothed it, almost as if she were patting a favorite pet, and then stacked them. She looked down at her hands as she said, "If there's anything else I can do to help you, I'd be honored."

"The honor is all mine, Trudy," he said. "I hear you're a natural-born artist with a needle, and your applique work is brilliant. I hope to see it at next year's quilt show."

"Thank you." She blushed and then finally found the nerve to look Matt directly in the eye. "I can't believe you know who I am."

"Dee and Emma have told me all about you."

"But you're *Matteo*. The face that launched a million trips."

"That's not really me." Now it was Matt's turn to blush, although his skin was much darker than fair Trudy's, so it was less visible. "I prefer to think of myself as an arts reporter."

"Oooh. Gorgeous and humble," Trudy whispered. "Just like in the ads."

"Time to get back to work now," Matt said, sounding a little more anxious than I'd ever heard him before. He didn't look at me as he picked up two pieces of fabric and stuffed them in front of the foot of the sewing machine.

I must have looked as confused as I felt, because Trudy explained, "You know. His videos were a viral sensation."

"I must have missed it." I'd been the epitome of someone living under a rock for the past ten years or so before I was forced to change careers, working eighty-plus-hour weeks and spending whatever free time I had studying quilts and hanging out with friends who apparently were living under their own rocks. Or perhaps it was just that we'd had so little time to spend together that we barely had time to share important things, let alone ephemera like internet celebrities. "I've never spent much time online except for checking court dockets, and those websites don't have any ads."

"But his face is *everywhere*," Trudy insisted. "He's the spokesmodel for an online travel agency that figured out that women make the majority of travel decisions, and they enjoy looking at a pretty face as much as men do. The agency went from obscurity to the top of the heap as soon as Matteo appeared in their advertising."

I stared at Matt. "Is that true? You weren't just a model, but a full-fledged celebrity?"

He shrugged, still not looking at me but keeping his attention on the fabric he was manipulating. "It's not that big a deal. It was an interesting experience, but I've moved on mostly. I only do the occasional special appearances now."

"I'm sorry," Trudy said, her face turning red and tears filling her eyes. "I didn't know you didn't want to talk about it. I'm so stupid. I should never have come today. I'm just making a mess of everything."

Matt abandoned his sewing and spoke gently. "You haven't made a mess of anything."

"Then why didn't Keely know all about your being a celebrity? You two are together, so if she didn't know, it's because you didn't want her to know. You were probably waiting to make sure she loved you for who you really are, not for being famous, and now I've ruined it."

"You didn't ruin anything." Now I was blushing at the thought of the entire quilt guild keeping tabs on my supposed relationship with Matt. "We only met recently."

"But we spent some real quality time together," Matt said, eyeing me defiantly. "Murder investigations tend to speed up the process of getting to know a person. At least the things that matter. We didn't talk much about my video work, because it wasn't that important."

"I'm so sorry." Trudy's tears began to fall.

"You really don't have to be," I said. "You didn't tell me anything that matters. I promise not to hold Matt's other life against him."

Trudy's tears only fell faster, and I didn't know how to convince her that she hadn't done anything wrong. If anyone was to blame, it was Matt for keeping secrets. He and I could straighten everything out between us later. For now, we needed to distract Trudy.

"Forget about Matt," I said, ignoring his anxiously affronted expression. I didn't mean it literally, but he deserved to stew a bit like I'd done for the past twelve weeks. "I've been meaning to ask to see your charm bracelet. Dee and Emma told me you've got quite a collection of thimbles on it."

Matt caught on right away, proving once again that he was more than just a pretty face. "How many different types of thimbles are there anyway?"

Trudy sniffled. "I'm still collecting them, but so far I've got twelve." She held out her wrist and started at the clasp, describing each charm in order. There was the standard thimble that everyone remembers from playing Monopoly. And then there were several variations on the same shape, but with openings at the tip for air circulation or on one side so the fingernail wouldn't be covered. There was a spoon-shaped one for using on the underneath finger to avoid pricks. And then there was one that looked a great deal like the one that had been found in the parking lot.

"Wait," I said. "Tell me more about that one."

"It's a leather thimble. Usually used on the bottom hand for the same protective reason as a spoon." She moved to the next thimble on her bracelet, which looked very similar, except there was a little circle where it would cover the pad of the finger. "If it's going to be used on the top hand, there's usually a metal reinforcement like this one has."

"I don't suppose you know anyone in the guild who uses a leather thimble," I said. "I'd love to see a demonstration of how it's used. I've never seen one before."

"Sorry. I've only been to a few guild meetings, and no one was doing any hand quilting during them, so I don't know who uses which thimble." Trudy brightened a little. "I can ask around for you."

Trudy's eagerness to help might bring a little too much attention to our interest in leather thimbles. "No, there's more-important work to do today. I'm sure Dee and Emma can arrange a demonstration when we're not so busy."

"Besides," Matt told her, "I need you to do something for me. You did say you'd help if I needed anything, right?"

She nodded.

"Good." Matt started explaining that he needed some fabric pieces that were slightly different from the standard sizes in the cutting table's baggies. It didn't make much sense to me, but Trudy nodded with obvious comprehension.

I tuned out their conversation while I reflected on this latest revelation. Matt had obviously left out a few little details when he'd first told me about his modeling career. He'd only shared the barest information, saying he'd quit at the peak of his career. I'd gotten the impression he had been a big deal within the fashion industry, but he hadn't said anything about being recognizable outside of it. A fashion model was a whole order of magnitude less recognizable than what he'd actually been, someone apparently famous enough to be known by just one name: Matteo.

I had to wonder what else he hadn't told me. Perhaps if he hadn't disappeared right after the quilt show, I might have found out before Trudy spilled the beans.

Still, it wasn't like I'd just found out he was a serial killer. It would take some time to get used to the idea of him as a celebrity, but I'd mingled with famous people before at bar association events. Of course, none of them had asked for a tour of my bank vault.

* * *

I realized Jayne was giving me the evil eye, so I decided I'd better get back to my gophering duties. On the way to the cutting table, I saw that Gil had finished chatting with Fred and had returned to mingling with the volunteers.

I thought about going over to see if Fred had heard anything new about the investigation, but just then he turned to peer out into the hall. A moment later Faria appeared with Stefan and Sunny, who headed straight for the back of the room and the ironing board they'd been assigned to earlier. They were wearing cheap, one-size-fits-many slippers, and Sunny's appliquéd smock had been replaced with a basic white T-shirt. Presumably, the confiscated clothes and shoes were being tested for blood spatter.

I made a quick tour of the room, delivering baggies and picking up blocks that needed to be ironed and then quilted. As I dropped some blocks on Stefan's ironing board, I saw Faria leaving again, this time escorting Matt out of the room. He was usually quick to assure people that he was just a simple arts reporter, but that didn't stop him from doing a good job when a more serious story fell in his lap, and he was probably going to ask at least as many questions as he answered.

Stefan followed my gaze. "I bet they'll let *him* leave. Celebrities get special treatment all the time, and it's the schmucks like me and Sunny who get stepped on."

"You know Matt isn't like that," I said. "He certainly didn't try to use his celebrity status to impress me. I didn't even know about it."

"You're right." Stefan watched Sunny iron the first of the blocks that I had delivered, and then he pulled me over to the line of chairs next to the wall. He dropped into one of them. "I didn't mean it. Matt may not care about living up to his potential, but you're right that he also doesn't take unfair advantage. It's just that I'm so worried about Sunny."

I took my time finding a comfortable position in the chair beside Stefan's. I knew better than to promise anyone that there was nothing to worry about. Unexpected and unfair bad things happened all the time. If Alan Miller had told me this morning that he was afraid he might be assaulted on his way out of the building, I'd have automatically reassured him that everything would be fine, the same way I used to calm all my anxious clients on the eve of a trial. I'd have told him that the museum was perfectly safe and nothing bad could possibly happen to him here. And I would have been completely and tragically wrong.

Still, I thought Stefan was worrying excessively. Unless maybe he'd picked up on some reason to be concerned during their official interview. "Did the detective say anything to Sunny during the interview that made her anxious?"

"They wouldn't let me sit with her during the interview," Stefan said angrily. "That's suspicious right there."

"Witnesses are always interviewed separately, so they can't coach each other or be influenced unintentionally. I was just wondering if she said anything to you about…I don't know. Perhaps reading her her rights or asking what she felt were leading and incriminating questions."

"Nothing like that," Stefan said, calmer now. "At least as far as I know. The detective said we couldn't talk about what we said in the interviews with each other, so we didn't. The only thing that worried me—and it wasn't bad enough that I felt I needed to insist on having you there—was that they kept coming back to asking me about the scissors Sunny had contributed to today's event. The detective wanted to know how many there were originally, whether she had any more in her car, that sort of thing."

"I saw Officer Faria collecting them earlier." I'd thought it was just the natural impulse of a patrol cop, nervous about so many potential weapons in a room he was responsible for overseeing. Perhaps there had been more to it.

"That's what I told Ohlsen," Stefan said. "Faria would know better than I would how many scissors there were."

I was confident Ohlsen already knew exactly how many pairs Faria had confiscated. That meant he was trying to figure out if one was missing. And that suggested he thought one had been used as a murder weapon.

Even if that was true, it didn't necessarily make Sunny the prime suspect. Anyone could have grabbed a pair of her scissors today. I'd seen them everywhere this morning, from the cutting tables to the sewing machines and even the ironing boards.

Stefan continued, "I also told him that Sunny would know exactly how many scissors she'd brought, because she's an excellent businesswoman. The only thing she wouldn't be able to account for is how many pairs might have been taken home, the same way people absently put a borrowed pen in their pocket. It happens during the shop's classes occasionally, and usually the scissors get returned as soon as the person realizes what she did. It's hardly ever intentional, and I wouldn't expect anyone here would have taken a pair on purpose. I mean, they're all volunteering their time to help out the museum. They're good people, not criminals."

"Good people commit crimes of passion." Still, I hoped Stefan was right, even as I was becoming more and more convinced that the killer was one of the people in this room. If Sunny's scissors really were the murder weapon, that certainly increased the odds that someone here had done it. The only other plausible explanation was that Alan had stolen one of the scissors, perhaps as a gift for his grandmother, and then the killer had taken them from him. Unfortunately, that could still have implicated a quilter. Sunny might have seen him with the scissors and confronted him about the theft. It was easier to imagine Jayne in a self-righteous fury, reclaiming the stolen scissors and provoking Alan into violence and then killing him with the weapon that was so conveniently right at hand.

"You need to relax," I said. "Your anxiety will only make Sunny more nervous, and then the police will start to wonder what she's so worried about."

"I can't relax," Stefan said. "I keep thinking about how the very same detective who's in charge of this case arrested the wrong person a few months ago. She hadn't done anything. They still arrested her."

"Ohlsen had been wrong then, but he wasn't entirely irrational. His suspect did have the means, motive, and opportunity to kill Randall Tremain." I wanted to say that wasn't true of Sunny, but unfortunately, I couldn't. Not honestly. Sunny did have means, motive, and opportunity in this case. She was used to working with sharp instruments, probably not just quilting tools but also medical devices, and could well have had a pair of her own custom-made scissors close at hand. She had a reason to be afraid of Alan Miller, which could lead to violence as a preemptive form of self-defense. And, since she had found the freshly dead body, it wasn't too much of a stretch to conclude she had also had the opportunity to kill him. Stefan didn't need to hear that line of reasoning though. "Anyone can make a mistake. I think Ohlsen learned from it, and this time there's no one pressuring him into making a hasty arrest."

"Are you sure?" Stefan asked

"As much as I can be while I'm stuck in here with all the rest of the witnesses," I said.

Sunny handed off a stack of ironed blocks to Trudy and came over to get Stefan. "Your turn," she told him, tugging him out of his chair and taking his place in it. "I need a break."

She watched him shuffle over to the ironing board, his pants hems dragging on the wood floor. She waited until he took up the iron to work on the latest pile of blocks that Trudy had delivered, and then she turned to me. "Do you know if they found the murder weapon?"

"Not as far as I know," I said. "I'm guessing it was one of your scissors."

She nodded. "I think so too. It was certainly something sharper than the bag of batting scraps that I was carrying." She looked relieved to be able to talk about the experience openly. Maintaining an upbeat facade for Stefan had to be draining. At least, that had been my experience while keeping my clients' spirits up over the long months of discovery leading up to the trial. My doctor had told me that the years of doing that for my clients could have contributed to my current tendency to pass out.

"If Alan was stabbed," I said, "shouldn't that exonerate you? If you'd done it, wouldn't you have been covered with blood?"

Sunny looked a little faint, reminding me that she'd gone into shock earlier from the sight of Alan's blood.

"I'm sorry," I said. "I forgot about your phobia."

"It's all right," Sunny said. "I'm not usually such a wimp that I can't even talk about blood. Back in school, I was fascinated by it. I read about it, listened to lectures about it, and wrote about it in exams. I was even okay with it in test tubes and under a microscope. It was a big surprise when I passed out the first time I saw it coming out of a real live person. I thought I'd get over it with practice, but it got worse instead of better."

I knew the feeling. I'd once thought I could control my syncope events with willpower. Instead, the stress of trying to avoid them only increased the likelihood that I'd lose consciousness. "Shock isn't something you can control. You did everything you could this morning by calling for help."

"I know, but I wish I could have done something for the young man. I'm pretty sure it was too late by the time I found him, but if I'd gotten any closer, I would have passed out, and that wouldn't have helped anyone."

"It might have given you an odd sort of alibi though. A person who passes out at the sight of blood isn't likely to stab anyone, or do anything that would risk getting blood on herself. Assuming, of course, that the killer was likely to get spattered."

"It's hard to tell how much blood the killer was exposed to. I'm pretty sure he'd have gotten some on his clothes, but it might not have been a huge amount. It depends on the cutting instrument and the angle of the cut." Sunny hugged her ribs and closed her eyes for a moment. "Maybe I'm not as good at talking about a real person's blood as I am with theoretical blood."

"I understand," I said. "I was just curious."

"I'm okay." Sunny opened her eyes again but continued to hold onto her ribs. "I wish I could be more helpful. All I remember is seeing the blood around his waist, soaking his shirt. I couldn't even tell you how many wounds there were or how long he'd been dead, let alone how much spatter there was."

"Can I ask one more bloody question?"

"Sure," she said gamely.

"Alan's quilt seems to be missing," I said. "What if it was between him and the killer when he was stabbed? Would it have absorbed all the blood?"

"The Tree of Life quilt? That would be such a shame, compounding the tragedy. Stefan pointed the quilt out to me when you were appraising it. Despite the wear and tear, it was lovely." Sunny shuddered. "The thing is, blood isn't just a wet puddle. It's got some pressure behind it. And it's sticky. It almost acts like a magnet, attracted to everything. I used to think that it was practically alive with a consciousness that made it seek me out, aware that I was so freaked out by it. Now all I can picture is the quilt's green trees on a blood-red background. I don't care how well it's cleaned. I'd never be able to look at it again if that's what happened to it."

"It's just speculation on my part," I said. "I'd like to believe Detective Ohlsen will be able to identify the killer by finding traces of blood on him even if the quilt absorbed most of the evidence."

Sunny brightened. "You're right. Even with the quilt, I'd expect there to be at least a little blood on the killer somewhere. Certainly on the hands. Unless he stabbed Alan through the quilt. All the police have to do is inspect us all for blood spatter, and they'll know I didn't do it."

I doubted it would be that simple, but there was no point in worrying Sunny. Stefan was already worried enough for both of them.

CHAPTER FIFTEEN

———

Sunny and I returned to the ironing board where Stefan was working.

"What's he doing here?" Stefan said, nodding at the doorway where Faria had just returned to the boardroom with Matt. Faria had already managed to irritate the easygoing Fred Fields, who pulled the pink-and-brown Cinnamon Sugar Bakery bag out of his pocket, peeked inside it to make sure it was empty, and then stalked over to the trash can next to the conference table to throw it out. "I don't trust the rookie."

I didn't either, but Faria was still a cop, and antagonizing anyone who had the power to make an arrest was foolish. It was an even worse idea in the midst of a murder investigation.

Faria caught sight of me and gestured for me to come over to the doorway.

"I'd better go see what he wants." I gathered up the handful of finished blocks from the end of the ironing board. "I'll drop these off on my way."

Faria waited impatiently while I left the blocks at the appropriate station for layering and basting. He was bouncing on his feet when I finally got to him. "Ohlsen sent me to get you. He needs an expert opinion on something he found, and he seems to think that's you."

Perhaps they'd found the Tree of Life Quilt. "What is it?"

"He wouldn't tell me. He didn't want you to be biased by my description, I guess."

More likely, I thought as I followed him into the hallway and down the back stairs, it was because they considered him as useless at a crime scene as I was at sewing. Despite his uniform, Faria was as much of a lowly gopher as I was today.

Detective Ohlsen was waiting for me just outside the back door. He was holding an evidence bag with a pair of scissors in it. He raised the bag to my eye level and demanded, "Recognize this?"

"They're scissors." The murder weapon, presumably. There were traces of what might otherwise have been rust, except that it was obvious the scissors were new and barely used. It was fortunate Sunny hadn't been asked to identify them. "I assume you know that though. More technically, they're eight-inch dressmaker's shears."

"Notice anything unusual about them?" he said.

"Not really. I'm an appraiser, not a quilter. All I can really tell you about scissors is that quilters use them, and they come in a variety of sizes and shapes. Individual quilters may prefer one size or style over others, but they're not as customized as the leather thimble you found earlier."

"This one is," Detective Ohlsen said. "It's engraved with *Sunny Patches*. Does that mean anything to you?"

My stomach churned. Maybe Stefan hadn't been worrying needlessly. I'd been right to guess that Alan had been stabbed with one of Sunny's scissors, and now it looked like they'd found the actual pair that had killed him. If so, the police now had something that might connect Sunny with the crime, not just with finding the body. "Sunny Kunik owns a quilt shop known as Sunny Patches."

"I know that much." Detective Ohlsen stared at the bag for several moments before saying, "I'm wondering how these scissors got tossed into the trash container."

"Sunny provided a lot of the supplies and tools for the ornament-making event in the museum today. She brought at least a dozen pairs of those scissors. I saw them all over the place in the boardroom. Anyone could have picked up one of them and carried it out here."

He grunted and stared at the evidence bag for long moments. Eventually, he looked up again and seemed surprised that I was still there. "It's a start, anyway. There might be prints on the scissors. And it means we were wrong about thinking he was killed by one of his buddies. Everyone in the boardroom is a suspect now."

Faria offered his opinion. "You've got to watch out for little old ladies when they get together. They can be vicious."

"I wouldn't be so quick to narrow down the possibilities." I thought Ohlsen was right, but it was never good to rush to a conclusion, and I really didn't want him to be focusing exclusively on Sunny. "From what I've heard, the victim had a history of shoplifting, and he was in the boardroom for at least an hour. He could have picked up a pair of the scissors, and I doubt anyone would have noticed one was missing, since there were so many of them. Then, if he got into an argument with the killer, he could have brandished the scissors, and the other person managed to get control of them."

Ohlsen considered it and then said, "Stranger-crime is less common than most people believe it is."

"It wouldn't have to be a stranger," I said. "Alan told me he needed to call someone to give him a ride home, and he had to go outside to make the call since there's no service in the boardroom. He came back inside for a while and then left again. The person giving him a ride could have killed him and then peeled on out of here before Sunny returned from her supply run."

"That's one theory," Ohlsen said, and his tone was too even to indicate whether he found it credible or not. "We've got the victim's phone, but it's password protected, so it'll take time to check his phone records."

"I think you're wasting time looking for another person," Faria said. "It's got to be one of the ladies in the museum. I'm telling you, I've seen how crazy they can be when it comes to their little hobby. Maybe one of them caught the guy stealing her scissors and decided to teach him a lesson."

Detective Ohlsen ignored the rookie's speculation and gestured for one of the forensic techs to get some gear and join us at the door to the museum. "We're going to have to take everyone's prints before anyone can leave. Just in case."

Much as I hated to believe that one of the quilting volunteers was responsible for taking a young man's life, I was becoming more and more convinced that it was true. There just wasn't any evidence to know for certain. The police needed something more than mere speculation.

There was the leather thimble, of course, but it probably wasn't even relevant. The forensics team had spread out across the entire parking lot, so for all I knew, they'd found it quite some distance from the body. But if it had been found close to his body...

"Before you start with the prints, could you tell me something?" I asked.

Ohlsen did his standard staring into space routine for a solid sixty seconds while he considered my question. "What do you want to know?"

"It's about the leather thimble," I said. "Maybe if I knew where it was found, I could find the owner more easily."

"I'm afraid it's going to be a while before you can return it to the owner." He looked disappointed by my question. Maybe he'd actually reconsidered the possibility that the thimble was related to the murder. "Your alibi checks out, so it can't hurt to tell you where it was, as long as you promise not to mention it to anyone else."

"I can keep a secret." It was a necessary prerequisite to practicing law, after all, and quilt owners seemed to expect the same level of confidentiality. I'd been amazed at all the personal information people volunteered during their appraisals.

"It was under the victim's leg. We found it when the body was taken away."

Given the isolated location of the crime scene, it seemed unlikely that any of the quilters would have had a reason to drop it there unless it had happened during a confrontation with Alan. Only the two or three people who'd parked at the far end of the lot—like Sunny—would have had any reason to be anywhere near the crime scene. That might be good news for Sunny. As far as I knew, she didn't actually sew, so she wouldn't own a thimble of any sort, let alone one as well used as the one being held as evidence. Her role in the quilting community was like mine, more of an interested observer and enabler than a practitioner.

"As long as you're going to take everyone's prints, there's something else you could check," I said. "Do you still have the leather thimble, or have you sent it back to the lab for processing?"

"It's still here, but we've got more important things to do than empty out the lost-and-found bin."

"What if the owner of the thimble was the killer?" I said, and quickly explained my theory about how isolated the crime scene was and how few people might have been near there for legitimate reasons.

Ohlsen considered it for longer than he'd considered whether to tell me where the thimble had been found. I waited as patiently as I could until he suddenly turned and called for a tech to go get the thimble from the forensic team's van.

He turned back to me. "You think I should have everyone try it on, I suppose. That sort of thing didn't work so well during the Trial of the Twentieth Century."

"They did it wrong," I said. "They should have known ahead of time whether the gloves fit. That's what pretrial discovery is for. Or the initial police investigation."

"I don't get it," Faria said, unable to contain his desire to be involved. "You think someone got killed over a stupid thimble?"

"It's just an idea," I said. "Not so much as a motive, but just another piece of forensic evidence, like a fingerprint. Something the killer happened to leave behind while committing the murder. I know that matching the thimble to the owner won't prove that its owner killed Alan, but if there's other evidence linking her to the victim, it might add up to enough for a conviction."

"You willing to prove your theory?" Detective Ohlsen said. "Be the first to try on the thimble?"

A regular thimble would fit a large number of people, but a custom one as well used as this one was had more in common with a DNA paternity test, where the odds of a match to anyone but a blood relative were infinitesimally small. There was virtually no chance the thimble would fit me, especially since I was taller and probably had larger hands than most of the quilters in the guild. It was bound to be too small for me, enough so that even a layperson would be able to tell. "Sure."

At a nod from Ohlsen, the returning tech gave me a pair of latex gloves that matched her own, and then she carefully removed the thimble from the evidence bag. Once I was properly gloved, the tech handed me the thimble. I slid it on the tip of the index finger of my left hand. To my surprise, given my relatively large skeleton, it dangled loosely. Whoever had owned it originally had an even larger hand, and it had fit the owner snugly, judging from the various irregularities in the leather where it had stretched to accommodate the raised finger pad and the hills and valleys between the base of the nail and the first joint of the finger.

"This is where most quilters wear a leather thimble while quilting. It protects the bottom hand from needle pricks." I slid it off the index finger and tried it on the middle finger of the same hand before demonstrating with the same two fingers of my right hand. "Sometimes they'll wear it on the middle finger, and if they're left handed, it would go on those fingers, but on other hand."

Ohlsen peered at my hand. "I'm guessing it shouldn't be that loose."

"No. It should be a snug fit. A little leeway is useful, to allow for the finger to swell in hot weather, so you should be able to turn the thimble like a person might do while fidgeting with a wedding ring." I spun the thimble on my finger. "It definitely shouldn't wobble like this. That would make it too difficult to keep it in place. It would be slipping off all the time."

Faria looked over my shoulder. "Whoever used that thimble is a man."

"Not necessarily. Anyone who works with her hands on a regular basis can develop strong fingers and calluses that would add to their overall size. Some of the older quilters probably have arthritis and would need a larger thimble to accommodate their swollen joints."

Still, Faria had a point. It made sense to start the testing with the males in the room. Carl was a large man, so he was a likely enough candidate, although he'd claimed that he didn't use a thimble. The only other men in the boardroom were Matt and Stefan. Even if I didn't know Matt had an alibi, I would discount him as a suspect. He had long, slender hands, not much wider than mine. I tried to remember what Stefan's hands looked like, but they were usually covered with his overly long sleeves. Most likely, they were as small and thin as his overall body structure.

Sunny's hands, strong from her physical therapy work, were probably larger than Stefan's.

Gil was taller and therefore likely larger handed than I was, so the thimble might come close to fitting her, although she should have video evidence of her whereabouts at the time of the murder to establish an alibi.

The tech reclaimed the thimble from me and tucked it safely back in the evidence bag. Ohlsen pondered his options again, staring at the museum's brick back wall without seeing it.

"This is stupid," Faria said. "We should be doing real police work, not playing with a sewing kit."

That seemed to help make up Ohlsen's mind. He pulled out his cell phone. "We're going to need more techs if we have to test the thimble on everyone and still clear the scene before dark."

* * *

Detective Ohlsen got Faria out from underfoot by sending him around to the front of the building so the officer who'd been turning back visitors and rubberneckers could take a break. Ohlsen had me wait while he collected three techs—two to take fingerprints and one to oversee the thimble testing. The plan was to move everyone out of the boardroom and into the hall and let the techs set up their equipment without alerting the witnesses to the thimble test until the last minute.

Once we returned to the boardroom, I noticed Carl was still working at one of the sewing machines in the front row. Since his size made him the most likely person to fit the large thimble, I said to Ohlsen, "Perhaps test Carl first?"

For once, Ohlsen didn't have to think about it. "Would you let him know we'd like him to stay behind while Officer Fields moves everyone else out into the hallway?"

I went over to the first sewing machine table. "They're planning to take everyone's prints, starting with you, if you don't mind. They'll probably let you leave after that if you want."

"I'm not an invalid," Carl said irritably. "I need to take it easy after the incident earlier, but that just means no physical exertion. Might as well stay here and get some work done while I'm stuck in a chair."

"How are you going to get home?" I'd given up my driver's license voluntarily because of the risk that I might pass out at the wheel. Carl probably shouldn't drive today either.

"I've got a ride." He nodded at a woman whose name I didn't know. "And Trudy offered to drive my car home for me. She's the only one here who knows how to drive a stick shift. I warned her she'd have to walk past the crime scene, since I'm parked practically in the far corner of the lot, but she said she'd manage. That young woman is a lot tougher than I gave her credit for."

The boardroom's double doors had just closed behind the last quilter when Fred poked his head back through them. "Keely, could you join us out here, please?"

I left Carl and headed out to the hall, where Ohlsen was explaining that the techs were preparing to take everyone's fingerprints. "It's completely voluntary at this point, but we'd appreciate everyone's cooperation. If anyone has any reservations at any point in the procedure, I'd be glad to talk with you privately." He looked down the line, making eye contact with each person, giving her or him the opportunity to speak up. A few looked away, but no one demanded either a private conversation or a lawyer.

"Very well," he said, opening the door behind him. "I'll go see if the equipment is set up."

As soon as he was out of sight, Stefan scurried over to me. "Can he do this?"

"You have the right to refuse," I said. "If you're worried about it, you can tell the detective that you want to talk to your lawyer first. On the other hand, doing that might make them take a closer look at you."

"Are you going to do it?"

I shrugged. "No reason for me to refuse. They've already got my prints in a database somewhere, from when I took the bar exam."

"I need to think about this," Stefan said. "If it was just me involved, I'd do it, but maybe Sunny should wait and talk to a lawyer, since they're probably already looking at her as the prime suspect. If she's going to refuse, then I will too."

"You could always go to the end of the line while you think about it," I said. "I don't mind going first, and maybe they'll find something useful before they get to you, and they won't need your prints."

"I'll go second," Gil said. "Under any other circumstances I'd probably refuse, just on principle, but I can't do that here and now. I need to show everyone—not just the police—that I've got nothing to hide. It's going to be hard enough explaining a murder on our property to the museum's board of directors and all our donors. The only way it could be worse is if anyone thought I might have had something to do with it."

"No one who knows you would ever believe you were a killer," I said. "Just don't start singing 'Mack the Knife' around Ohlsen. He doesn't have much of a sense of humor, and I have no idea what his musical tastes are."

Gil groaned. "Now I've got that song running around in my head. I'm blaming you if I get distracted and start singing it."

"Everyone always blames the lawyer," I said.

From somewhere in the middle of the crowd, Trudy pushed her way over to where Fred Fields stood blocking the doors. She drew herself up to her full height, which was somewhat above Fred's, and announced, "It's not right, fingerprinting innocent people, making us feel like criminals. I'm not going to do it. I'll get a lawyer if I have to."

"I'm sorry you feel that way, miss," Fred said. "Just wait in the back of the line for now, and if you change your mind in the meantime, that's fine. If not, I'll let the detective know that you've decided not to help us find the person who killed that poor young man."

"He wasn't a poor young man. He was horrible." Her surprising assertiveness faded almost as quickly as it had appeared. "I'm sorry. It's not that I don't want to help. I just don't want my fingerprints on record anywhere. These days, you never know who will end up with them, and there's no privacy anymore. I didn't kill anyone, and I wasn't anywhere near the corpse where I might have touched something, so taking my prints is just a waste of time."

Jayne's shrill voice preceded her as she pushed her way to the front of the crowd. "How long is this going to take, anyway? We've wasted at least half an hour coming out here while the equipment is being set up. How hard is it to open up a few ink pads and set out the index cards? We could be making more ornaments instead of standing out here in the hall doing nothing."

Meg emerged from the crowd to say, "I'm sure everyone's doing their best. Jayne, perhaps you could be one of the first to be fingerprinted, right after Gil, and then if they let you stay in the room, you can organize everyone into finishing the last of the ornaments. If we concentrate all our effort on the ones that are partly done, instead of starting any more, we should be able to finish quite a few."

"But you're the featured instructor," Jayne said. "I'm just the assistant. You should go in before me."

"I would, but I'm afraid I need to visit the ladies' room again. Then when I come back, someone needs to stay out here and keep everyone calm." Meg looked at Fred. "Do you mind if I make a quick trip?"

Fred deputized Gil to stand at the door to the boardroom and keep anyone from going inside until the techs were ready. Fred went with Meg to the openings for the two stairwells, which led in one direction to the museum lobby, and in the other to the back parking lot. Meg continued along the hallway while Fred stayed behind where he could keep an eye on both the ladies' room door on one side of the stairwells and the quilters outside the boardroom on the other side.

I turned to see how Dee and Emma were doing. They were standing at the end of the hall, beyond Stefan and Trudy even, having a fiercely whispered conversation. What were they planning now? Even if it had mostly been a joke, I had promised Gil I'd keep them out of trouble during the police investigation, so I went over to check on them. They stopped arguing before I could make out their words.

Emma gave me a grateful look. "Dee wants to refuse to give her prints, like Trudy did."

"I'm eighty-three years old, and I've never had so much as a speeding ticket," Dee said. "No way I'm getting added to the criminal justice system at this point in my life. Not after what happened to dear Emma last spring."

"That's certainly your right." Arguing with Dee would only make her more set on her plans. All I could do was try to minimize the damage. I glanced at where Trudy was huddled nearby on the floor with her back against the wall. "I'm sure Trudy would enjoy the moral support. She looks a little scared after her big stand against authority. I assume Emma will also refuse in solidarity with you, so the three of you can keep each other company until the detective gets a court order. You should be home by midnight with a little luck."

"Midnight?" Dee said, some of her defiance fading like Trudy's had.

"More or less." The reality of how slowly the legal system could grind might change Dee's mind. I explained as we walked over to join Trudy. "It will take a while to get the warrant application together and figure out how to establish that they've got reasonable cause. If they're lucky and can find a prosecutor to present the request for them on a Saturday afternoon, it shouldn't be hard to get it approved. They'll still have to find out which judge is on call for emergencies and arrange to meet somewhere to make their argument and get his signature. Depending on the judge's mood, he might insist on hearing them close to where he lives, which could be some distance from here. Then they need to process the paperwork back at the station and finally bring it out here to serve on you. So midnight, more or less. Possibly into the wee hours of tomorrow. Shouldn't be longer than that though. You'll be home in time for church. Probably."

"I don't care if I have to pull an all-nighter," Dee said with renewed defiance. "Trudy's got it right. Taking innocent people's fingerprints is just wrong."

"I can't stay overnight," Trudy whispered. "My family would be worried."

"I'm sure they'll let you make a phone call," I said.

"Oh. Good." Trudy didn't sound even a little bit reassured.

"You can claim my phone call too if you need to make more than one," Dee said. "Keely can call my granddaughter to let her know I'm fine. Did you know they used to work together? Lindsay introduced us to Keely."

"Really?" Trudy looked less scared now that she had an ally.

"Really." Dee leaned against the wall next to the young woman. "It's a good thing too. She was a big help a few months ago when we needed a good lawyer."

One of the boardroom's doors was opening, and everyone in the hall took a couple of steps backward, looking down at their shuffling feet like young students who were unprepared and hoping that if they didn't look at the teacher, they wouldn't get called on. The nervousness was only going to get worse as reluctant witnesses were dragged—metaphorically, if not physically—into the boardroom. That kind of stress could be contagious, something I really didn't need to be exposed to, and it would only make the process take longer.

I scooted over to the doors to tell Ohlsen in a voice loud enough that everyone in the hall could hear that I'd be glad to go first with the fingerprinting. I wasn't just doing it to reassure everyone else. I also wanted to find out whether the thimble had fit Carl. If so, Ohlsen would gather all the evidence anyway, just to prevent a defense attorney from claiming the thimble might have fit someone else as well, but there wouldn't be much question left in anyone's mind about the actual culprit.

Gil was right on my heels in the line forming outside the doors. Matt ambled over to join us, beating out Jayne, who was a few steps behind him. Jayne might not be happy about setting an example for the others, but she was still obediently following her idol's orders.

The detective took me, Gil, and Matt inside, leaving Jayne behind for now. Fred returned with Meg in time to block Jayne from peering through the crack between the doors.

Inside the boardroom, the techs had removed the sewing machines from the first long table and had set up three adjoining stations, the first one with the leather thimble and a stack of latex gloves, the next one for fingerprinting, and the last one to scan for blood spatter.

Carl had been moved to the back desk where I'd done appraisals this morning. Ohlsen went over to the tech at the thimble station and said, "Well?"

The tech shook his head. "Didn't fit. It was sort of the right size, or at least it didn't swim on him like it did on Ms. Fairchild, but the contours were all in the wrong places."

I skipped the thimble station, since I'd already established it didn't fit me, and went straight to the first fingerprinting setup. To distract myself from the automatic tendency to interfere with the tech's methodical placement of my fingers across the scanner, I watched Gil trying on the thimble. Even from a few feet away, I could tell it didn't fit.

My relief turned to curiosity. Who else could the thimble possibly fit? Gil was the tallest woman in the museum today, with proportionately large bones, so if anyone's fingers were large enough for that thimble, it should have been Gil. The only person here today who might have larger bones was Matt, who was right behind Gil. The tech had him slip it on each of his middle and index fingers. It wasn't a bad fit at the tip, but flared out much too wide as it approached the first joint. The tech glanced at me, as if seeking my opinion, and I shook my head. The excess leather at the knuckle would have made the thimble more irritating than helpful.

Four suspects down, about thirty to go.

CHAPTER SIXTEEN

————

Carl was being interviewed at the back desk by Detective Ohlsen, and the tech supervising the thimble fittings radioed for Fred to send in the next three witnesses. Jayne strode over to the first station, where she immediately began arguing with the tech. Her shrill voice reached all the way to the back of the room, where Matt and I kept Gil company while she waited to be interviewed by Ohlsen. The tech who had taken Gil's prints had told her that the processed witnesses were supposed to stay in the boardroom, so it would be easy to keep track of who'd finished the testing and who still needed to be printed. I suspected it was also so that no one would ruin the surprise of the thimble by spilling the secret to the quilters still waiting in the hallway.

"What was that thimble test all about?" Gil said.

"Probably nothing important." Until she gave her statement, I couldn't tell her anything substantive. "They're just being thorough."

"That's not what I wanted to hear," Gil said. "I was hoping you'd tell me they were going to pull some Perry Mason trick and identify the killer with absolute certainty by her thimble."

"Or *his* thimble," Matt said. "Carl and I just proved that men are capable of wearing thimbles too."

There was one other man to test, assuming he didn't insist on waiting for his attorney. "I wonder if Stefan knows how to use a thimble."

"As of about six months ago, Stefan hadn't done any more sewing than you have," Gil said. "But he's been spending a lot of time at his girlfriend's shop lately, so he might have picked up some new skills."

I watched Jayne and the next two quilters as they were tested, half expecting the tech at the thimble station to shout some code phrase after finding a match, so Fred would come running into the boardroom to take the suspect straight to Ohlsen for more intensive questioning and probably a Miranda warning. I couldn't seem to look away from the tech stations, until I caught a glimpse of Matt and Gil in my peripheral vision, one on either side of me. They too were mesmerized by the testing process.

There had to be something more useful we could do than to watch the testing. I forced myself to look away from the spectacle and then lightly elbowed both Gil and Matt to get their attention.

"What's the parallel saying to *a watched kettle never boils*, for forensics work?"

"How about *slow and steady wins the trial*?" Matt suggested. "Or perhaps *fingerprint in haste, repent at leisure*?"

Gil looked away from the techs and their subjects. "I just feel so helpless sitting here. How could someone get killed right here on the museum's property? And what are our donors going to think when it hits the news that there was a murder on the premises? They're going to think the museum is in a bad neighborhood, not the sort of place they want to be associated with or give money to."

I recalled Gil mentioning a new donor who'd made a sizeable contribution, one that had covered the expenses of today's event, as well as funding the local quilt registry. "Are you worried about your new major donor?"

Gil glanced at Matt, and he shook his head.

I'd seen that sort of exchange before when Matt hadn't wanted me to know he'd been a model before becoming a reporter. What was he hiding now? Was he the new major donor? If so, how had he found time to arrange it, when he'd been out of town for the last twelve weeks?

"I'm not worried about him reneging on his pledge," Gil said. "But other donors might, and the museum depends on them for our day-to-day expenses. We're a small museum, no real endowment to speak of. Losing even a few of our consistent donors could be the beginning of the end. Not just for my job and your contract for the quilt appraisals, but for the museum itself. When word gets out that longtime donors are dropping out, no one else will want to contribute."

My stomach was starting to churn in sympathy for Gil's obvious distress, but one thing I was trying to do better for controlling my stress levels was to not dwell on worst-case scenarios that might never happen. "They can't blame you for a murder you didn't commit."

"That's the thing about being the person in charge," Gil said sadly. "I'm ultimately responsible, so they can blame me for everything. You know how it goes: the buck stops here."

The room was filling up as more and more quilters went through the forensics gauntlet, trying on the thimble. As far as I could tell, none of them had come close to having fingers of the right size and shape. It was starting to look like it had belonged to one of the quilters who'd left before Alan did, and it had simply been dropped on his or her way in or out, rather than during the murder. Possibly whoever had parked in the far corner of the lot before Sunny did.

I consoled myself with the reminder that the thimble had been a long shot, something of a shortcut, but not the only way to find the killer. I had to believe that Ohlsen would find another way to close the case, clearing Gil and the museum of any responsibility. "Ohlsen is a good detective. You really don't have anything to worry about in the long run."

"Time isn't my friend here," Gil said, apparently too anxious even to find an appropriate bit of lyrics to sing. "If the arrest isn't in the same headline with the murder, it'll be too late. Charitable donors are notoriously fickle and easy to scare off. I was hoping to really impress the board and our donors with the holiday events this year. Looks like I'll be making an impression, all right, just not a good one. Even if the scandal doesn't land the museum in serious financial trouble, there will definitely be cutbacks. Probably starting with the quilt acquisition program. You and Stefan are going to feel the cuts."

"Don't worry about us." I hadn't expected to make a profit with my appraisal business for another year or two, and I was actually doing a bit better financially than I'd anticipated, thanks to both Gil and the Danger Cove Quilt Guild enthusiastically spreading the word about my services. I was fortunate too, to still have a healthy nest egg from my years as a lawyer. I was more concerned about the toll it would take on Sunny if the investigation dragged on. I was certain the thimble wouldn't fit her, but unless it fit someone else, Sunny was likely to remain at the top of the list of suspects. "Stefan will be happy as long as Sunny isn't arrested, and I collected a number of leads on new clients today, so I'll be fine."

"Hey," Matt said. "How come no one's worried about me? I could lose my job as a reporter if I keep ending up at major crime scenes without getting much of a scoop."

I snorted. "You can always go back to being an internet sensation. It must pay considerably better than small-town journalism."

"It's not all about the money," he said. "I like being an arts reporter. Or at least I did until people started dying all around me."

"Maybe you should retire from journalism," I said. "The cops are going to start wondering if you're a serial killer, and you're too pretty to go to jail."

"I didn't think you'd noticed."

Oh, I'd definitely noticed back in August. But before I could do more than simply be aware of Matt, his pretty face and all the rest of him had disappeared without a word.

* * *

Jayne was bearing down on us, so I left to collect some blocks that needed ironing, Gil waited to be called up for her interview, and Matt loped over to claim the sewing machine next to Carl again and throw himself into the work. I didn't know why he was so anxious to avoid Jayne; he could charm any woman on the planet. And it wasn't just about sexual attraction. He could charm most of the men he met too.

Jayne caught up with me at the table where three women were layering blocks with batting and backing. "What's taking the cops so long? It's past the time when Meg planned to leave, and she's got a long drive home to the far side of Seattle. The guild can't afford to pay for her to stay another night at the Ocean View B&B, and we can't expect her to pay for it out of her own pocket. She's already been incredibly generous with her time, especially since she's doing this event for free instead of charging her usual rates."

"Some things can't be rushed," I said. "Think of a murder investigation as comparable to making a quilt. The work needs to be done right if a person's going to be sent to prison for life. That means it takes whatever time it needs to take."

She grimaced. "We all know there are only two possibilities. It's got to be either Carl or Sunny. The rest of us should be allowed to leave."

Jayne might be annoying, but she also had traits that would have made her a good detective. She was smart, and she paid attention to detail.

"Why those two in particular?"

"It's obvious," she said. "Carl's little medical incident was just too convenient, which makes me think he did it on purpose to avoid being questioned."

That didn't seem at all likely to me. Carl hadn't appreciated being the center of attention when Meg had praised him, and I knew from personal experience just how embarrassing it was to pass out in public. Carl would never have done anything to bring attention to his weakness, least of all when someone like Richie Faria was around to carry tales back to the rest of the police department. Besides, I'd seen how anxious Carl's service dog was before he passed out. I didn't think that could have been faked.

"And what about Sunny? Is it just because she found the body?"

"That was just what got me considering her initially," Jayne said. "Then the more I thought about it, the less it made sense that she'd been so freaked out by finding him. She's a nurse, so she must have seen dead bodies before. The hysterics had to have been an act. And why would she fake her reaction other than to cover up the fact that she'd killed him? She was fine when Carl needed help. If she were the type to panic, she should have been screaming then too."

I could have explained that the difference was that Carl's emergency was bloodless, but I wasn't sure how well known Sunny's blood phobia was, and it really wasn't any of Jayne's business. Besides, I only had Sunny's word for the blood phobia. Her reactions out in the parking lot had seemed real enough to me. Of course, as a nurse, Sunny would know exactly what the symptoms of shock were, so she could fake them, at least well enough to fool a casual observer like me. The paramedics might have questioned her condition, but they still probably would have recommended standard treatment for shock even in the absence of objective findings, just as a safety precaution. Otherwise they might find themselves in the witness stand with someone like myself—before I retired, of course—grilling them on standard practice for treating a witness to a traumatic event and why they hadn't followed it in this case.

Much as I hated to admit that Jayne could be right, I wasn't absolutely sure that neither Carl nor Sunny had killed Alan Miller.

* * *

When Jayne finally let me get back to work, the techs were packing up their gear, and I realized that everyone who'd agreed to be fingerprinted had completed the process. Meg was encouraging the quilters to keep making ornaments, Gil was reassuring anyone who appeared anxious, and Jayne was undoing all their work by making everyone tense again. As far as I could tell, only Trudy, Sunny, Stefan, Dee, and Emma were still out in the hall with Fred Fields, having apparently stuck to their decision to wait for a warrant before being fingerprinted.

At the interview desk, Ohlsen raised his phone to his ear. A moment later, he stood and left the room. Before the door closed behind him, I caught a glimpse of Fred Fields out in the hall, keeping an eye on the last few recalcitrant witnesses. As long as Meg didn't need to be escorted to the ladies' room again, Fred's presence in the hallway was sufficient to keep us all under lockdown. It wasn't as if anyone could really make a run for freedom—there were officers stationed at the two exits downstairs, and there was nowhere to hide from the surveillance cameras on the first floor. There were windows in Gil's office and the adjoining break room for employees, but even though we were only on the second floor, the building's high ceilings downstairs made the distance to the ground more comparable to being on a standard third floor. Anyone jumping out a window would be lucky to only break her arms and legs and not her neck and back. She certainly wouldn't be in any condition to run away.

Shortly after the doors closed, they opened again, and Fred appeared to call me out into the hallway. I dropped off the freshly ironed blocks I'd been transporting and went into the hall. I'd been right. Only Trudy, Sunny, Stefan, Dee, and Emma were still out there, seated on the floor in the far corner of the hallway, holding hands to demonstrate their solidarity. Ohlsen was nowhere in sight.

Fred silently walked me away from the remaining witnesses, past the stairwells, in the direction of the restroom until we were out of casual hearing range. He turned so he could keep an eye on his charges and then spoke, his voice low and worried. "I don't like the way things are going here. I think Ohlsen's stumped and just going through the motions."

"I assume the thimble didn't fit anyone."

"Too big mostly," he said, nodding. "A few times they thought they might have had a match in terms of circumference, but it was lumpy in the wrong places. They didn't even have enough to hold anyone for further questioning, and now they've got a new theory. They're taking another look at Sunny, since she's refused to be printed, and she was of interest anyway as the person who found the body."

Crap. Stefan had been right to worry. "She wasn't the only one who refused."

"The others aren't likely suspects. Dee and Emma have alibis, credible ones, not just vouching for each other. Besides, I think Bud's a little bit nervous about going after either of them after the uproar the last time."

"What about Trudy?" I didn't want to cause her any trouble, but she didn't have an alibi, and she'd admitted to being in the parking lot during the time after Alan left. The police needed to consider all the possibilities, even though it was hard to imagine the easily cowed young woman stabbing someone. Then again, Trudy had been much more assertive when she'd refused the fingerprinting. If Alan had provoked her sufficiently, who knew what she might have done? "It's not often that someone has the courage to say no to the police, which makes me wonder if she's got something to hide."

"Oh, we know why she refused," Fred said dismissively. "She told me she's got psoriasis, and she's afraid the fingerprinting process will cause a painful flare-up. She even showed me a prescription ointment in her purse, and I looked it up. The only thing it's ever prescribed for is psoriasis. She can't be exposed to the scanner or the gloves we're using. We've got special equipment and allergy-free gloves at the station for that sort of thing, and she agreed to go there after we're done here. That just leaves the woman who found the body as the prime suspect."

Stefan was going to blame me for this development, and there wasn't much I could do about it. Butterflies started flitting around my stomach. Feeling helpless was a major cause of stress, worse than outright conflict.

"Sunny Kunik didn't kill anyone," I said.

"You sound awfully certain."

"I am." Or at least I was trying to convince myself that I was certain. "For one thing, she doesn't have a motive, unless it was self-defense, and in that case, she didn't have any reason to lie about stabbing Alan. The fact that the victim had been harassing her was well documented, so it wouldn't have been difficult to prove self-defense. For another thing, she's got a blood phobia. She'd have passed out if she'd cut him, but she was fully conscious when Matt and I got out to the parking lot."

"I was hoping you'd say she had an ironclad alibi," Fred said.

"Hardly any suspect truly has a solid alibi that can't be challenged in court," I said. "It's too bad the thimble didn't fit anyone. That might have given Ohlsen a solid lead. The only other useful piece of evidence is the missing Tree of Life quilt. If you could find that, I think you'd know who killed Alan. He was carrying it when I saw him leave, and it had considerable sentimental value for him. He wouldn't have simply tossed it away or given it up easily."

"You think he might have been killed for it?"

I headed off the question of the quilt's value. "I was thinking more in terms of the killer using it to clean the blood from his hands and then hiding it in case there was forensic evidence on it that would identify the killer. Maybe he got cut too, so some of the blood belongs to the killer. Find the quilt, and you'll find the guilty person."

"All I know is that the quilt wasn't anywhere in plain sight," Fred said. "To really look for it, Bud will need a warrant to search the museum and the vehicles in the parking lot."

"He'd better get working on it then." Ohlsen had probably started the process already, to go along with the warrant to gather the remaining fingerprints. "No one's going to complain too much about being cooped up in the boardroom as long as they've got the ornaments to keep them busy, but the event was supposed to be over in about an hour, and people probably have plans for the evening. It won't be long until people start demanding phone calls and legal representation."

"I'll see if the warrant's on its way." Fred stuck his hand into his jacket pocket to pull out his phone and came out with only a napkin from the Cinnamon Sugar Bakery. He sighed before using his free hand to pat down the rest of his jacket and pants pockets, which fortunately weren't as numerous as Matt's.

Fred finally found his phone, but instead of dialing it immediately, he took a moment to stare at the pink-and-brown napkin. Finally, he stuffed the reminder of his addiction to sweets back where he'd found it. "I need a break."

"Not as much as Ohlsen needs a break in this investigation."

CHAPTER SEVENTEEN

———

Fred stayed where he was to make his call, and I went over to see how the conscientious objectors were doing. Someone had gotten them chairs, apparently deciding wisely there was no chance that mere discomfort would make Dee change her mind about her fingerprints, and it wouldn't look good to keep an eighty-three-year-old woman seated on the hard floor for hours on end.

Dee and Emma had the two middle chairs, with Sunny and Stefan on one side of them, and Trudy, looking miserable, on the other. She must have felt guilty about having given in to the pressure to be fingerprinted, because she'd scooted her chair about a foot away from the others and turned sideways on the chair with her back to them, like a toddler who believed that if she couldn't see them, they couldn't see her.

"Well?" Dee asked. "Have they found a match yet?"

"It doesn't work that way," I said. "Fingerprint matching isn't quite the science that TV and the movies make it seem. It's a slow process. I don't know exactly how long it takes for this police department, but it will definitely be days rather than minutes. And that's assuming they got clear prints from the murder weapon."

Trudy turned in her chair to face us. "They found the murder weapon?"

"They believe so."

"I bet it was a pair of scissors." Trudy slumped deeper into her chair. "Maybe I'd better call a lawyer. My prints are probably on all of the scissors in the room. Sunny brought enough for everyone to have her own pair, but you know how it is. You can never find your tools when you need them. People were always asking me to get them scissors. Even Jayne thought that was one job I could do reasonably well, although she did take one pair away from me and stick it in her back pocket. I think she was just looking for an excuse to tell someone not to run with scissors. I wasn't, really. I just have long legs, so I move pretty fast even when I'm walking."

"It sounds like there'd be multiple sets of prints on any of the scissors you handled, and they were probably smudged by whoever used them after you did. Even if they can find your prints along with others, they'd have to have a reason to suspect you instead of the owners of the other prints. Something like a motive for wanting Alan dead."

"That's the problem," Trudy said. "I do have a motive. Sort of. I mean, I wouldn't actually kill anyone, but I knew Alan Miller. We went to high school together. He had a crush on me, and he wouldn't leave me alone when I said I wasn't interested in him. Really freaked me out by following me around town. He still does…I mean, he still did it all the time. At least, it felt that way. I'm not sure if he was following me exactly, but it's a small town, and he'd see me somewhere and come over and tell me how pretty I was, and how I'd look even better in tight clothes, and how come my boyfriend wasn't with me? That sort of thing. Every single time he saw me."

"Did you ever get a restraining order against him?"

Trudy shook her downcast head. "I was afraid it would just make him do something worse."

"It would be hard for the police to think you went from doing absolutely nothing about his bothering you to suddenly killing him," I said. "It would be different if you had a long history of police involvement or you'd ever threatened him with violence if he wouldn't leave you alone."

"Well…" Trudy sighed. "There was this one time, when I was out window-shopping here on Main Street a few months ago, and Alan started following me and saying stupid things. I saw a cop coming out of the Cinnamon Sugar Bakery, and I ran over to see if he could help me." She nodded in the direction of Fred Fields, who was still just out of hearing range, talking on his phone. "It was the same cop who's watching over us today. I told him what was happening, but when I turned around to point out Alan, he was gone. I don't know if the cop will even remember."

Another cop might not, but Fred would definitely remember. The only thing I wasn't sure about was whether he'd mentioned it to Ohlsen yet. Fred might not think Trudy was a viable suspect, but Ohlsen would if he knew about the history between Alan and Trudy. And now I was starting to wonder about Trudy too. She was such a timid young woman, but I couldn't help thinking about the old saying that still waters ran deep.

* * *

The conscientious objectors were fine and didn't need me to hold their hands, so I headed back inside the boardroom to see if there was something useful I could do.

The quilters were getting restless as the work was wrapping up. Only two of the workstations were still operating: the one for quilting through the three layers of the miniature quilts, and the one with the machine that attached the binding and hanging loop. There were only about a dozen ornaments left to be layered at the first station, and the woman doing the binding was finishing them as fast as they were arriving at her table.

Jayne stood over the basket of the finished ornaments now, acting as a self-appointed quality-control inspector. She snatched the latest addition out of the basket and announced, "This is unacceptable. The hanging loop has some exposed raw edges. It needs to be ripped out and redone."

The woman who had made the offending loop acted as if she hadn't heard Jayne's shrill voice and picked up the next little quilt that needed binding.

Meg, on the other hand, must have heard the complaint, since she hurried over to intervene. She took the supposedly defective ornament from Jayne. "Oh, that's not so bad. I bet you could fix it with a few hand stitches and a little tuck in the binding."

"It wouldn't look good on close inspection," Jayne said.

"That's all right," Meg said. "These little quilts aren't going to be in a juried show or anything. No one will ever notice once it's hung on the tree."

"A quilt judge would notice."

"Not after you've worked your magic on it, especially if it's placed high on the tree, where no one can get a close look at it." Meg steered Jayne over to the abandoned cutting table. In addition to the rulers and rotary cutters, there was a pincushion, three sizes of cheap metal thimbles, and two spools of thread— one red and one white.

"I guess a temporary repair will do for now," Jayne said. "After the holidays, I'll take the worst ones home and do them right."

"Make sure to let the museum's director know that you're not stealing them," Meg said, "just fixing them."

Curious to see how the little imperfection would be hidden, I followed to watch as Jayne threaded a needle, created a tuck in the binding fabric, and then folded it over the tiny bit of raw-edged fabric that stuck out. Her stitches were so tiny they appeared to be part of the binding fabric. When she reached the bottom of the loop, where it met the top corner of the quilted ornament, the needle got stuck in the thick layers. Jayne grabbed the largest of the thimbles and stuck it on the tip of her thumb. It was too small, barely covering the tip of her thumb, but it was enough to allow her to push the needle past the sticking point.

And then it dawned on me. I knew why the leather thimble hadn't fit anyone during the tests. It wasn't designed for a finger; it had been worn by someone who used her thumb to quilt. It wasn't a common method, but I'd seen it a few times during my studies. That would explain why it was too big even for the largest-boned people in the room, Carl and Gil, and it had only fit the tip of Matt's fingers, flaring out too far at the knuckle.

Ohlsen needed to try the thimble on everyone in the room again, but wearing it on thumbs instead of fingers. This time, I suspected it would be noticeably too small for Carl, Gil, and Matt. I couldn't tell just by looking at Jayne's thumb whether it would match the leather thimble, but she'd just jumped to the top of the suspect list. She was easily angered, she had no alibi, and she'd given a false name when questioned by the police. Dee and Emma had said Jayne could get violent, at least to the extent of property damage, over quilting issues, and she'd admitted to being irritated with Alan Miller for his mistreatment of the Tree of Life quilt. Jayne's perfectionism might have an even darker side than what anyone had observed so far. I'd heard often enough during my stress support group meetings that perfectionism could be a killer, but until now I'd never thought the saying might be true in a literal sense.

I needed to let Ohlsen know that we'd been looking at the thimble all wrong, and that it might yet be the key to identifying Alan's killer.

CHAPTER EIGHTEEN

————

Ohlsen hadn't returned to the boardroom, so I told the female officer at the door that I needed to talk to Fred, and she let me past without the hassle Faria would have given me.

Outside, the hallway was deserted, only the five empty chairs remaining at the near end of the hallway to indicate where the conscientious objectors had been seated. Fred must have been instructed to take them downstairs for transport to the police station. Apparently someone had forgotten to tell the officer inside the boardroom.

I was debating whether I should continue down the back stairs on my own, when Meg slipped through the doors behind me.

She smiled wryly. "You know where I need to go."

"Officer Fields has left," I said. "You'll have to let the officer inside know you're out here alone."

"I can't wait that long." Meg was doing the restless little dance of someone who really couldn't wait.

Talking to Ohlsen, on the other hand, could wait a couple of minutes.

"I'll go with you." If anyone questioned our being outside the boardroom, we could vouch for each other. It wasn't like either one of us was going to make a run for freedom, and even if we did, there were officers at each of the exits, prepared to stop us.

"Oh, thank you, thank you, thank you," Meg said, her grateful smile making her look even more the very image of Mrs. Claus, even without her pinafore apron and red hat.

"No problem," I said.

We reached the point in the hallway where it was open to the two sets of stairs, one to the museum lobby and one to the parking lot. Meg glanced in both directions, as if at a stop sign, looking for oncoming traffic. The tension on her face deepened the lines around her eyes and on her forehead. Perhaps she was afraid of heights. The stairs were steeper than in more modern buildings and seemed to go on forever.

To distract her, I said, "Doesn't your bladder condition interfere with your more formal teaching events? I would think the students would get restless if the instructor keeps having to leave in the middle of an explanation."

"That's why it's so important to have a highly trained assistant," Meg said, continuing past the stairwells. "Jayne helps out whenever she's able to attend an event, and most of the time she's better at my techniques than I am. I was her very first instructor, and she soaked up everything I had to teach. I sometimes wonder if she might have gone in a different direction with her quilts if she'd latched on to a different instructor. She decided that whatever I did was the only right way to do things, and everything else was inferior."

My stomach lurched, the way it did when I was in the beginning stage of a stressful situation, before the nausea and light-headedness that presaged passing out. Usually, I knew exactly why my symptoms appeared, but there didn't seem to be any reason right now. Ohlsen had shown himself willing to listen to my insights today, I'd at least solved the mystery of the thimble to my satisfaction, and I even had a good idea of who was going to turn out to be the prime suspect. It would be particularly interesting to see how Jayne explained why she hadn't claimed the thimble when she'd first seen it in the hands of the forensics tech.

But something was wrong, my body kept insisting. Nausea rose, and I leaned against the wall halfway between the stairwell and the door to the ladies' room.

What on earth was going on with my nervous system?

One of the most frustrating aspects of a syncope event was that my thinking tended to go fuzzy as soon as the stress began, which then clouded my judgment and made it more difficult for me to think of a way to avoid the stress. A little cold water splashed on my face might help me to concentrate. I needed to be able to think straight when I got downstairs and told Ohlsen my latest insight about the thimble and its likely owner.

Meg stopped to peer at me anxiously. "Are you all right?"

"Nothing serious, but I think I'll use the ladies' room after you."

"I'm used to people following in my footsteps," Meg said with a self-deprecatory smile. "Usually, it's in quilting techniques though, not bladder control."

I needed to stop thinking about the nausea and concentrate on something pleasant and soothing. Like a whole room full of quilters copying Meg's quilting techniques while creating amazing works of art for me to appreciate. I pictured Jayne and Trudy and Dee and Emma and even Stefan, all lined up, mimicking their instructor. First, the cutting, then the stitching and ironing and machine quilting. And finally a few hand stitches to secure the hanging loop, using their thumbs to push the needle through the thick layers of fabric.

As the image came into focus, I sucked in a startled gulp of air. Had Jayne been copying Meg when she used the thimble on her thumb? If so, that put Meg right up at the top of the suspect list with Jayne. Meg had no alibi for the time of Alan's murder. She'd claimed she was in the ladies' room when Sunny screamed, but I had no way of telling if that was true. Meg had definitely had the means to do the murder; I'd seen her put a pair of Sunny's scissors in the pinafore apron. I'd thought she'd discarded the apron and hat as inappropriate for the aftermath of the murder, but there could have been another reason for getting rid of it: it had Alan's blood on it.

Perhaps most damning of all, Meg had tried on the thimble exactly as directed, fighting the muscle memory that, assuming I was right about where Jayne had learned to use a thimble, would have automatically called for wearing it on the thumb. If I was wrong, and Jayne hadn't learned that technique from her favorite teacher, Meg still would have known that Jayne used a thimble on her thumb, and I thought Meg was enough of a natural-born teacher that she wouldn't have been able to help herself from sharing that information with the forensic tech.

The only thing missing was motive. Why on earth would Meg have killed anyone, least of all a young, down-on-his-luck guy trying to do a nice thing for his grandmother? Without some explanation for why she might have wanted Alan dead, it would be difficult to convince Detective Ohlsen to search Meg's vehicle for the missing quilt and the pinafore apron. Especially since now I was working more from intuition—and the evidence of my hypersensitive nervous system—than from logic.

I wasn't even sure I could explain my theory well enough for Ohlsen to take me seriously, not with my head swimming.

"I really need to go," Meg said. "Will you be all right here by yourself?"

It hadn't been that long since Meg's last trip to the bathroom. Less time than any of her previous trips, I thought.

There was something other than her bladder behind her urgency. I needed to stall until I could figure out what was going on.

"Just give me a minute for my head to clear."

Meg glanced in the direction of the ladies' room, but she didn't leave me. Either she was truly concerned about me or she knew it would be suspicious if she acted too callously.

If she didn't actually need to use the toilet, why was she so desperate to get to the restroom? What if she had stashed evidence of her guilt there? Like her pinafore, which surely would have had at least some of Alan's blood on it if she'd stabbed him. Meg could have tossed the scissors in the trash, stowed the quilt in her car, and headed back inside the museum before she realized she was wearing incriminating evidence. Even if someone had seen her dashing toward the ladies' room to get rid of it, no one would have thought anything of her actions.

If I was right about Meg being the killer, then the apron had to be in the ladies' room, and I had to keep her from destroying it. Gil would definitely give the police permission to search there, so no warrant was necessary. Then forensic testing would confirm that the blood had belonged to Alan Miller.

"You know," I said, "perhaps we should go back to the boardroom so I can sit down before I end up needing paramedics."

Meg transformed suddenly, no longer looking even remotely like Mrs. Claus, unless Santa had married a vicious serial killer. Her eyes were narrowed, and she reached out to grab me by my arm. I tried to pull away from her, but I was too light headed and dizzy to free myself.

It was probably a good thing that Faria had confiscated all the scissors as soon as he'd arrived. Except he hadn't thought to confiscate the rotary cutters, and Meg had just pulled one out of the back of her waistband, where it had been stowed like a gangster's illegal gun.

I froze long enough to confirm that the safety guard had been retracted and the blade was fully exposed.

I took a step backward, but Meg followed, shoving the rotary cutter toward my face and forcing me to continue backing up. Unfortunately, if I kept going, I'd be in a precarious position between the two stairwells. One good shove and I'd go tumbling down the steep stairs.

At least now I knew who had killed Alan Miller. Of course, that wasn't particularly comforting now that she was threatening me with a sharp blade. She'd probably intended to cut up the bloody apron and flush it down the toilet, and that was why she'd smuggled the rotary cutter out of the boardroom. Now, it was coming in useful for making sure I couldn't alert the police before she destroyed the evidence.

She had a weapon, but I had the advantage of height and relative youth. I planted my feet and refused to move any closer to the stairwell. My arms were longer than hers, so I had a reasonable chance of keeping her from hitting anything vital with the rotary cutter. Anything was better than a fall down those steep stairs.

"As long as we're not going anywhere," I said, "why don't you tell me why you did it?"

"Did what?"

"It's over," I said, bluffing. "Before Fred left, he set up an appointment for me to talk to Ohlsen, so the detective is expecting me in the parking lot. I should have been down there by now, and he's not a patient person. He's going to come looking for me in a minute. When he gets here, I'm going to tell him that you killed Alan Miller, and if he tries the thimble on your thumb, it's going to fit you better than the proverbial leather glove. Plus, I'm going to tell him that your apron is hidden somewhere in the ladies' room up here and that they'll find Alan Miller's blood on it."

"You're wrong." Meg waved the rotary cutter at me again.

I took a cautious sideways step, trying to force her to trade places with me so she would be closer to the stairs than I was. I had to move slowly, so as not to provoke a further attack from Meg and also to prevent my light-headedness from worsening. Meg might not even need to push me down the stairs if I got too close and my nervous system did the job for her, causing me to pass out at just the wrong time and place. I needed to remain calm. And vertical.

Easier said than done, in the circumstances.

"I'm not wrong about you," I said. "The only thing I don't understand is why you did it. Everyone seems to admire you and appreciate how generous you are toward your home town."

Meg shook her head and laughed bitterly. "It's true, you know, what they say about not being able to go home. Too many ghosts, too much unfinished business."

"Alan was just a kid when you left Danger Cove," I said. "You couldn't possibly have had any problems with him."

"Not with Alan directly. With his family," Meg said. "You're an outsider, so you don't know. The locals know. Ask anyone. The McLaughlins and the Millers were practically family to each other for generations. My mother and his grandmother would have considered each other BFFs if they'd had texting and Twitter back when they were growing up together."

"That would make Alan something like a cousin," I said. "I know families can have their arguments, but that doesn't explain why you'd want to kill him."

"There's more to it," Meg said. "My mother and his grandmother were best friends, but they were also complete opposites. We McLaughlins have always had a reputation for working hard and succeeding. The Millers have pretty much the opposite reputation. Not that they're lazy exactly, but no matter how hard they work, they still fail at whatever they set out to do. Only my mother didn't care. She accepted them as they were."

"Again, I don't understand," I said. "Perhaps there are mitigating circumstances, and I can let the detective know, but only if I understand, and I don't. You've just confused me even more. You killed a friend of your family."

Meg's laughter grew even more bitter. "That's the thing. They weren't really our friends. All this time I thought they were, and it was a lie. My mother, bless her soul, is gone now and doesn't have to learn the truth. The friends she cherished all her life had actually betrayed her."

"Not Alan," I said.

"Oh yes, he did," Meg said. "He lied to me. He said his grandmother made the Tree of Life quilt."

I did some quick mental math. "Assuming his grandmother is around fifty years older than he is, she could have made it when she was in her early twenties. The materials and design are right for that era, and it's got an embroidered date to confirm it."

"You got the date right," Meg said. "But it wasn't made by Alan's grandmother. It was made by my mother. You probably noticed that it wasn't a scrap quilt. It was made of five green prints and just one red print. All bought new. My mother scrimped and saved to buy that fabric before the first Christmas of her marriage. She was determined that her children would have a special quilt just to be used in December. It was supposed to be a tradition to be passed down through the family."

The longer I could keep Meg talking, the better the chance that the officer inside the boardroom would wonder what was taking us so long and come out to check on us. "Your mother sounds like a wonderful, caring person. I still don't understand how her tradition became a motive for murder."

"That quilt should have been mine," Meg said fiercely. "I would have taken care of it. Those Millers never took care of anything. I saw what they'd done to the quilt. It was a mess of stains and tears and broken stitches. My mother would have been heartbroken if she'd known how it would end up. She always stored it away from January to the end of November, and then she only brought it out in December, when we took turns sleeping under it. I still remember the first time I was old enough to be entrusted with it."

"Still," I said, "you can't blame Alan for what his family did."

"You don't understand. It should have been mine. He stole it."

"Alan did?" I said. "He didn't seem to have any particular attachment to it other than that it belonged to his grandmother."

"Another lie," Meg said. "I suppose I should have said that his grandmother stole it. All these years, and we never knew. See, it disappeared during my mother's wake. She died a few weeks after Christmas one year, and she'd been too sick to remember to put the quilt away. It was on my bed still. Maybe I should have folded it up and put it away on my own, but I was only twelve at the time, and I knew my mother was dying. The quilt helped me to cope, since I knew I'd inherit it someday, and I'd always have it to remind me of her."

I was beginning to understand. All this time, Meg had felt guilty for not putting the quilt away properly, and then she'd seen it today and realized who had stolen it. All of her guilt had turned to rage against the family that had caused her so many years of distress. "So you followed Alan out to the parking lot to demand that he return your property, and things got out of hand. I can see how that could have happened."

"It wasn't just the quilt," Meg said. "I recognized it at once, of course, and I was going to wait until after today's event was over, and then I'd go file a police report. But the more I thought about it, the angrier I got. Not so much at the initial theft of the quilt, but at the ongoing betrayal. Decades of it. I can still remember Alan's grandmother comforting me over the loss of the quilt. She even helped me look for it when we thought it had just been misplaced. Everyone thought she was being such a good person, taking time out of her busy schedule to honor the friend she'd just lost. And all along, the woman had actually stolen it. It wasn't some random thief who took it. She knew how much the quilt meant to my mother and the whole family. She *knew*, and she took it anyway."

I couldn't help saying, "I'm sorry." It really had been a terrible betrayal.

Meg didn't seem to hear me. "The least they could have done was to take care of the quilt, but oh, no, they treated it with as little respect as they showed our friendship. They took it and abused it."

I suspected there was another explanation. The damage to the quilt wasn't as extensive as it could have been if it had been mistreated. The wear and tear was consistent with reasonably careful but constant, everyday use over several decades. Alan Miller hadn't seemed like a bad kid, despite his rap sheet and his harassment of Trudy. Rather than coming from a family of cold-hearted liars, it was just as likely that Alan's grandmother had been grieving when Meg's mother died, and she'd "borrowed" the quilt on the spur of the moment during the wake, for much the same reason that Meg had left it on her bed beyond the holiday season: for the memories it held. And then the situation had gotten out of hand, and there had been no easy way for Alan's grandmother to return it.

Meg was too far gone with reliving her anger to stop now. "I tried to reason with him, explain that the quilt didn't belong to his grandmother, but he wouldn't believe me. Said his Gran would never steal anything, that she'd almost disowned him once for his shoplifting. He might have convinced the cops to let him keep the quilt if they'd heard his lies, but I knew better. He was just like everyone else in his family. He was evil through and through. People thought the Millers were the unluckiest family in town, but now I know they were just getting what they deserved."

As Meg relived the morning's events, she forgot to keep the rotary cutter poised to threaten me. Now was my chance.

I took a deep breath and prayed that a sudden move wouldn't be the last straw for my nervous system, and shoved Meg down the hallway, away from the stairwells, tackling her as hard as I could. We both fell onto the floor.

Meg was so startled that I was able to knock the rotary cutter out of her hand and send it careening down the wood floor before she realized what was happening. She went limp, and for a moment I thought she might have hit her head when we fell, but her chest was rising and falling. The struggle seemed to have gone out of her. I didn't trust her enough to roll off her though. I wasn't sure what she might do to me, or possibly to herself. As long as I kept her here, someone would eventually come looking for us. Besides, my head was swimming, and I wasn't sure I'd be able to stand up right now. Fortunately, she didn't know that.

"Where's the quilt now?" I said gently, hoping to get an answer while she was so wrapped up in her anger that she didn't realize how incriminating it would be.

Meg didn't say anything for long moments, much like Detective Ohlsen's prolonged silences while he mulled over a bit of evidence. Finally, she said, "If I tell you, will you do me a favor?"

"If I can."

"I know you're going to turn me in to the police, but would you explain to them why I did it? That I didn't mean to hurt anyone, but that the quilt meant so much to me that I just snapped. They'll listen to you, and you understand how people can get so attached to a family quilt."

I did understand. It wasn't the quilt itself that had set her off, but what it stood for, both the good memories of Meg's mother and then the bad memories of loss and heartbreak. That was true of all heirlooms, but in this case, it was an even stronger trigger, since it epitomized all the years of betrayal, the feeling that people who were supposed to be her friends had actually been keeping a secret from her, possibly laughing behind her back over her trust in them. "I can't promise they'll understand, but I'll do my best to explain."

"Thank you. It's in the trunk of my car." Meg took a deep breath. "One more thing. Would you make sure the quilt is taken care of when it's released from evidence?"

"That will be up to whoever ends up owning it. It sounds like you have a claim to it, but I'm guessing that Alan's grandmother is going to claim she's the legal owner." I didn't add that Meg was unlikely to be in any position to sue for possession of the quilt. She was going to have enough legal problems dealing with the murder charges.

"Just promise me that if you can do anything to make sure it's preserved, you will," Meg said. "My mother only made a couple of other quilts, and they were meant for daily use, so they fell apart years ago. This is the only one that survived."

"I'll do whatever I can." I thought it was safe now for me to get to my feet without passing out and without Meg doing something crazy. I stood and held out a hand to pull her up.

"Before we go talk to the detective, I really do need to use the ladies' room." Meg took my hand. "After you collect the apron from the ceiling tile where I stashed it, of course."

CHAPTER NINETEEN

———

Two weeks later, everything at the Danger Cove Historical Museum was as perfect as I could have wished.

Gil was dancing around the lobby singing "O Tannenbaum," alternating between English and German lyrics, while she waited for Dee to throw the switch that powered the strings of lights on the tree in the middle of the room. The mayor, Edward Kallakala, was mingling with his constituents at what had turned into Danger Cove's premiere social event of the season, and Elizabeth Ashby was keeping to the edges of the crowds, observing everyone and writing in her red-and-green notebook. Even Carl Quincy was there with his service dog.

The background music faded, the ceiling lights dimmed, and the twenty-foot tree sparkled with twinkling white lights, dozens of miniature wooden lighthouses, and hundreds of the red-and-white quilted ornaments. Apparently some of the quilt guild members had continued to make them at home until yesterday, when volunteers on ladders had hung them all.

A discreet sign next to the tree announced that there would be an auction to sell the ornaments on the Saturday after New Year's. According to Gil, the high preregistration numbers for the event were dancing in the heads of the museum's board of directors with more sparkle and allure than the more traditional visions of sugarplums. I had the Scrooge-like thought that the interest in the ornaments might have had more to do with the public's fascination with anything associated with murder than with an appreciation for either miniature quilts or the museum. Trying to hold on to the spirit of the season, I reminded myself that regardless of the buyers' motives, the money was going to a good cause.

Once the oohing and ahing over the tree had subsided, Gil called out for everyone's attention. "I promise not to keep you away from the refreshments much longer, but I have to thank everyone who worked on the ornaments for the tree."

There was a round of polite applause for the volunteers, and then Gil continued. "I also have a surprise announcement. You all know about the tragedy that occurred here a few weeks ago. It was a sad day for the town, the museum, and the quilting community. We can't undo what happened, and there's nothing that will take away the pain of that day for anyone who was involved. Still, I'm honored to announce that the Tree of Life quilt, made by Meg McLaughlin's mother, Sally McLaughlin, and subsequently preserved by Georgia Miller, has been donated to the museum."

A collective appreciative gasp filled the room.

"I know it will be difficult to look at the quilt without thinking of the tragedy surrounding it. But tragedy is part of life, part of art, and part of the discussion that a museum should enable. I, for one, am looking forward to that discussion and encourage you all to watch for an announcement that the quilt has been released by the police to our custody. Jayne Conners has offered to do the necessary restoration work on the quilt, and we all know how amazing her craftsmanship is. When she's done, we'll have a special exhibit inspired by the people who made and cherished the quilt."

Excited but solemn chatter erupted until Gil continued. "I'd be remiss if I didn't mention that you can be among the first to know of the exhibit if you find us on Facebook or follow us on Twitter."

Gil ended her announcements with a reminder that there were refreshments set up along the back wall of the lobby, and there was a rush for the buffet table, where I suspected Officer Fred Fields would be first in line. He was here today unofficially and not in uniform, although there was something about his personality that made his civilian clothes—dark-blue trousers with a pale-blue button-down shirt and a navy bomber jacket—look like a uniform.

Gil danced over to me in time with the background music. "I hope you don't mind that I didn't mention your involvement in solving Alan Miller's murder. You already know how grateful I am, and I didn't think it was the kind of publicity you wanted for your appraisal business."

"I don't know," I said in a teasing tone. "My schedule has been surprisingly full the last couple of weeks. Perhaps I should start advertising that I include a free murder investigation with every appraisal."

"It wouldn't be that much of a stretch, linking quilts with death," Gil said, surprisingly serious. "I don't know as much about textile history as you do, but I've read enough to know that many quilts were associated with death. They were made by or for people who were fighting a terminal illness or made to commemorate a death. I even read about one famous quilt where the center of it depicted a graveyard, complete with coffins labeled with deceased family members."

"I've seen pictures of that quilt," I said. "And it's not like the coffins were a way for a serial killer to keep track of her victims."

Gil laughed. "Are you sure? Perhaps the police missed it, just like they would have missed Meg's connection to Alan Miller if you hadn't gotten involved."

"Maybe after the holidays I'll look into it," I said. "The coffin quilt was from the early eighteen hundreds, so I don't have to worry about being threatened by the killer, if there was one."

Stefan, with Sunny beside him, interrupted to tell Gil that a potential new donor wanted to talk to her. Gil headed off to introduce herself to a white-haired man in black jeans with an expensive-looking jacket and tie.

"Thank you for…" Stefan glanced at Sunny. "For doing what you promised to do. I knew I could count on you."

Sunny gave Stefan a playful punch in the arm. "You don't have to be all mysterious about it. I know you were worried about me and asked Keely to watch out for me. You've got to stop being so protective of me."

"No, I don't," Stefan said with a big grin. He reached out and grabbed Sunny's left hand to display the antique diamond engagement ring on her finger. "This says I'm entitled to protect you just as much as you're entitled to protect me."

"Congratulations," I said.

"We're not actually getting married until next year," Sunny said. "It will take that long to get everything just right."

If anyone could arrange a perfect wedding, Sunny and Stefan could do it.

"We're keeping the celebration small, but you'll be on the guest list," Stefan said. "It's the least we can do after you helped keep Sunny out of jail."

Sunny reclaimed her hand. "You might not want to mention my going to jail too often or too loudly. People might get the wrong idea, and I am trying to run a small business here."

"No one would ever think you belonged in jail," Stefan said, completely ignoring the fact that he'd been afraid of just that when he'd begged me for help.

"Enough talk about jail," Sunny said. "Before Stef distracted me, I wanted to talk to you about participating in a new project at the quilt shop. We're working with the museum and the guild to make a reproduction of the Tree of Life quilt. We'll be raffling it off to raise funds for the museum. Don't worry—it will be clearly marked as a reproduction, right on the backing where it can't be removed by someone trying to pass it off as an antique. We thought you might want to help make it."

"I'm not much of a quilter," I said.

"You only need basic sewing skills," Sunny said. "Trudy has already volunteered to do all the really fussy work."

"Even so, I've been told I don't even know how to iron properly." I was tempted to ask if Jayne had agreed to help too, in which case I would prefer to stay far away. It was kind of her to offer to do the conservation work on the original Tree of Life, especially in light of her mentor's downfall. Someone else might have been a bit humbled by the experience—I'd heard that Jayne had quickly found someone else to serve as the source of the one true way to quilt and was still the same shrill, judgmental, and hypercritical person she'd been before. I definitely didn't need to be around that kind of stress.

The reproduction project was for a good cause though, and I doubted I'd ever get over my need to help people, even if I couldn't do it in a courtroom any longer. "How about if I help with choosing appropriate fabrics for the era, and I'll donate my time for an appraisal at the end to document it?"

Sunny turned to Stefan. "I told you she'd want to help."

"I know," he said. "I should have listened to you. You're always right. I'll try to remember that from now on."

"You can start by coming with me over to the buffet line." Sunny smiled and hooked her arm in his. "I told you the line would get too long if we came over to talk to Keely first, and look, it's longer than the tree is tall."

Stefan mumbled an apology as he let Sunny drag him toward the refreshments.

I was going to join them, except Matt appeared and offered me a mug of mulled cider. For once, he was wearing regular black wool pants and a button-down white shirt instead of his usual cargo pants paired with an oddly colored sport shirt.

Stefan had a valid point about Matt not living up to his potential most of the time, at least when it came to his appearance. He did clean up nicely. I had to wonder why he'd bothered though. Even if I was right that he was the new major donor for the museum, the one who had financed the local quilt registry for quilts with ties to Danger Cove, he wasn't the sort to brag about it. No, more likely Gil had probably convinced him to be here, looking like the online celebrity he was, knowing his presence would distract people from the recent tragic events.

"So," he said, "about that bank vault."

"What about it?" I still wasn't convinced he meant anything by his flirting. Sure, he'd been out of the country for the last twelve weeks, but with modern technology, that was no excuse for not contacting me. At a minimum, he could have sent a brief text from even the most remote areas of the world.

"So I'm still in the doghouse." He sipped his own mug of cider. "Maybe I can buy my way out with a tidbit of information you might find interesting about one of the people suspected of Alan's murder."

"And how would an arts reporter know anything about that?"

"A reporter never reveals his sources," Matt said. "It's about Jayne Conners. I bet you thought she was the killer. I certainly did."

"Just wishful thinking," I said. Jayne wasn't a bad person, so I was glad I'd never had a chance to confide my suspicions about her to Matt or anyone else. I'd told him about overhearing her give the police a false name, but not until after Meg was arrested, when we all knew Jayne hadn't killed anyone.

"Okay, tell me what you know about Jayne, and if it's good enough, we can talk about my bank vault."

"I know why she gave the cops a false name," he said. "She had an outstanding warrant, mostly for being stubborn, as only she can be. She'd ended up in a confrontation with a cop, claiming he was harassing her, because of course she never does anything wrong. She wasn't worried about her fingerprints leading to the warrant, because she figured that would take some time, and she could be taking care of the problem. She just wanted to buy herself some time for the police to find the killer before her name popped up in an outstanding warrant search."

"Okay, that's pretty good information," I conceded. "There's one more thing I need to know before I decide whether it's safe to let you into my vault."

"Sure, anything," Matt said. "If I don't have the answer, I'm sure I can get one. I am a reporter, after all."

"This won't require any investigation. I just want to know where you disappeared to after the quilt show."

"I didn't disappear. In fact, almost the exact opposite. Back before we met, I'd been negotiating with my old client, the travel website, to do a publicity tour that they could live stream." He gestured toward the case where the registry of Danger Cove quilts was stored. "One of the terms was that my fee had to be given to the museum, and for some reason that made it complicated. I got the call during the quilt show that they'd finally agreed to all my terms and wanted me on a plane that afternoon. Three months on the road, starting the next day. The events were live streamed, and snippets of them went viral. I figured you'd see me online and know where I was."

He couldn't have known that I avoided the internet as much as possible, since it was a known stress inducer. I tried to limit its use to reading my email and doing focused searches for information related to my appraisals, while carefully avoiding the chaos of advertising and newsfeeds and assorted internet kerfuffles.

It struck me that Matt had a lot in common with the quilts I appraised. In both cases, the first impression was based entirely on a pleasing appearance, but a closer examination revealed so much more—both good and bad. In a quilt, the imperfections were actually part of what made it so appealing, and I thought the same might be true of Matt.

He might not be perfect, but neither was I—no matter how much I tried. He deserved another chance to show that he meant it when he said he'd call me.

"Are you negotiating any other deals that would prevent you from visiting the bank vault in the near future?"

"Not a one," he said with a smile that could definitely launch a thousand trips.

ABOUT THE AUTHORS

Gin Jones became a *USA Today* bestselling author after too many years of being a lawyer who specialized in ghostwriting for other lawyers. She much prefers writing fiction, since she isn't bound by boring facts and she can indulge her sense of humor without any risk of getting thrown into jail for contempt of court. In her spare time, Gin makes quilts, grows garlic, and advocates for rare disease patients.

To learn more about Gin, visit her online at:
www.ginjones.com

Elizabeth Ashby was born and raised in Danger Cove and now uses her literary talent to tell stories about the town she knows and loves. Ms. Ashby has penned several Danger Cove Mysteries, which are published by Gemma Halliday Publishing. While she does admit to taking some poetic license in her storytelling, she loves to incorporate the real people and places of her hometown into her stories. She says anyone who visits Danger Cove is fair game for her poisoned pen, so tourists beware! When she's not writing, Ms. Ashby enjoys gardening, taking long walks along the Pacific coastline, and curling up with a hot cup of tea, her cat, Sherlock, and a thrilling novel. She is also completely fictional.

If you enjoyed this book, be sure to pick up the next
Danger Cove Mystery:

KILLER COLADA
Danger Cove Mysteries book #8

It's been a stressful couple of months for bartender, Hope Foster,
so her best friend Ruby treats her to an afternoon of holistic
pampering with therapist Pandora Williams. But what should be
a relaxing getaway turns into a murder scene when Hope and
Ruby stumble across Pandora's lifeless body in the kitchen next
to a killer cocktail.

www.GemmaHallidayPublishing.com